Winning His "Y": A Story of School Athletics

Ralph Henry Barbour

ESPRIOS DIGITAL PUBLISHING

WINNING HIS "Y"

BY RALPH HENRY BARBOUR.

Each Illustrated, 12mo, Cloth, $1.50.

Double Play.

Forward Pass!

The Spirit of the School.

Four in Camp.

Four Afoot.

Four Afloat.

The Arrival of Jimpson.

Behind the Line.

Captain of the Crew.

For the Honor of the School.

The Half-Back.

On Your Mark.

Weatherby's Inning.

D. APPLETON & COMPANY, NEW YORK.

"Gerald drew ahead steadily."

WINNING HIS "Y"

A STORY OF SCHOOL ATHLETICS

By

RALPH HENRY BARBOUR

AUTHOR OF
"THE SPIRIT OF THE SCHOOL," "THE HALF BACK,"
"FORWARD PASS," "DOUBLE PLAY," ETC.

ILLUSTRATED

NEW YORK AND LONDON
D. APPLETON AND COMPANY
1910

Copyright, 1910, by

D. APPLETON AND COMPANY

Published September, 1910

TO
GEORGE OSBORNE FORREST

CONTENTS

CHAPTER

I. — GERALD EVENS OLD SCORES

II. — HILTZ ENTERS A PROTEST

III. — WHICH MAY BE SKIPPED

IV. — POETRY AND POLITICS

V. — DAN BUYS A TICKET

VI. — CONDUCTING A CAMPAIGN

VII. — THE ELECTION

VIII. — AT SOUND VIEW

IX. — THE CROSS-COUNTRY MEET

X. — AT THE FINISH

XI. — BY ONE POINT

XII. — OFF TO BROADWOOD

XIII. — "FIGHTING FOR OLD YARDLEY"

XIV. — Around the Bonfire

XV. — The New Captain Makes a Speech

XVI. — The Picnic

XVII. — The Return

XVIII. — Building The Rink

XIX. — The Hockey Team At Work

XX. — First Blood For Yardley

XXI. — The Basket Ball Game

XXII. — Gerald Goes On An Errand

XXIII. — The Cup Disappears

XXIV. — Gerald Watches

XXV. — The Cup Is Found

XXVI. — Winning His "Y"

LIST OF ILLUSTRATIONS

"Gerald drew ahead steadily" *Frontispiece*

"'I guess I won't go, thanks,' said Dan"

"'Don't take the rug away yet,' begged Alf"

"His wide, startled eyes held Gerald's for a long moment"

CHAPTER I
GERALD EVENS OLD SCORES

"All together! Cheer on cheer!
  Now we're charging down the field!
See how Broadwood pales with fear,
  Knowing we will never yield!
Wave on high your banner blue,
Cheer for comrades staunch and true;
We are here to die or do,
  Fighting for old Yardley!"

They sang it at the top of their voices as they came down the hill, arm in arm, and crossed the meadow toward the village. There was no one to hear, and they wouldn't have cared if there had been. Tom Dyer sang the bass, Alf Loring the tenor and Dan Vinton whatever was most convenient, since about the best he could do in a musical way was to make a noise. It was a glorious morning, in the middle of October, and there was a frosty nip in the air that made one want to sing or dance, and as they were in a hurry and dancing would have delayed them, they sang.

"That's a bully song, Dan," said Alf. "You ought to think of another verse, though, something with more ginger in it. How's this:

"'We will knock them full of dents
  And we'll send them home in splints?'"

"Rotten," growled Tom. "It doesn't rhyme."

"It doesn't have to rhyme," said Alf. "It's poetic license."

"Well, you're no poet. What you need is a dog license, Alf!"

"He's just peeved because he didn't think of it himself," explained Alf to Dan. "He's one of the most envious dubs in school. Personally I consider it a very pretty sentiment and just chock-full of—er—poetic feeling. And I won't charge you a cent for it, Dan; it's yours. No, no, not a word! I won't be thanked."

"Don't worry, you won't be," said Tom. "If you put that in the song, Dan, I'll stop playing, and howl!"

"That might be a good idea," responded Alf. "I'll bet you'd cut more ice howling than you would playing, Tom."

"I'll try and think of another verse," said Dan. "But I don't think I'll work in anything about dents and splints, Alf. Besides, that doesn't sound very well coming from the captain. Remember that you're a gentleman."

"He knows better than that; don't you?" said Tom.

"I know I'll roll you around in the dust if you don't shut up, you old Pudding Head!" answered Alf truculently.

"Come on, you fellows," interrupted Dan. "We haven't any time for scrapping if we're going to get there to see the start."

"How far do they run?" asked Tom.

"About three miles," replied Dan, as he climbed the fence and jumped down into the road. "They start at the corner beyond the bridge, take the Broadwood road and circle back beyond Greenburg and finish at the bridge again."

"Is that the route when they run against Broadwood?" Alf inquired as they went on toward the Wissining station.

"Yes, only then they'll start at the Cider Mill and finish a mile beyond toward Broadwood, and that makes it a mile longer."

"Suppose little Geraldine will have any show?"

"I don't know, Alf. He's been at it ever since school began, though. He asked me if I thought he could make a cross-country runner and I told him to go ahead and try. I knew it wouldn't do him a bit of harm, anyway, and he was sort of sore because Bendix wouldn't pass him for football."

"Bendix was right, too," said Tom. "Gerald's too young and weak to tackle football."

"He's fifteen," objected Alf, "and, as for being weak, well, I know he handed me some nasty jabs in the gym last week when we boxed. They didn't *feel* weak."

Winning His "Y": A Story of School Athletics

"His father didn't want him to play this fall," said Dan, "and I'm glad he's not going to. If he got hurt, Mr. Pennimore would sort of hold me to blame, I guess."

"Glad I'm not responsible for that kid," laughed Alf. "You'll have your hands full by next year, Dan."

"Oh, he will be able to look after himself pretty soon, I fancy. They haven't started yet; let's get a move on."

They hurried their pace past the station and across the bridge which spans the river just beyond and connects Wissining with Greenburg. Anyone meeting them would, I think, have given them more than a second glance, for one doesn't often encounter three finer examples of the American schoolboy. Dan Vinton was in his second year at Yardley Hall School and was sixteen years of age. He was tall and somewhat lean, although by lean I don't mean what he himself would have called "skinny." He had brown eyes, at once steady and alert, a very straight, well-formed nose, a strong chin and a mouth that usually held a quiet smile. He was in the Second Class this year and, like his companions, was a member of the football team, playing at right end.

Alfred Loring was eighteen, a member of the First Class, captain of the eleven and of the hockey team. He was scarcely an inch taller than Dan, in spite of his advantage in age, and, like Dan, hadn't an ounce of superfluous flesh on his well-built frame. He had a merry, careless face, snapping dark brown eyes, an aquiline nose and hair which he wore parted in the middle and brushed closely to his head. He was as good a quarter-back as Yardley had ever had and this year, with Alf at the head of the team, the school expected great things.

Tom Dyer, his roommate, was a big, rangy, powerful-looking chap, rather silent, rather sleepy looking, with features that didn't make for beauty. But he had nice gray eyes and a pleasant smile and was one of the best-hearted fellows in school. Tom was captain of the basket-ball team, a First Class man and in age was Alf's senior by two months. All three of them were dressed in old trousers and sweaters that had seen much use, and all three wore on the backs of their heads the little dark-blue caps with the white Y's that in school heraldry proclaimed them members of the Yardley Hall Football Team.

A short distance beyond the bridge, on the outskirts of Greenburg, they joined a throng of some eighty or ninety boys. Of this number some thirty or so were attired for running and were engaged in keeping warm by walking or trotting around in circles or slapping their legs. The trio responded to greetings as they pushed through the crowd. Andy Ryan, the little sandy-haired, green-eyed trainer, was in charge of the proceedings and was calling names from a list which he held in his hand.

"All right now, byes," he announced. "You know the way. The first twelve to finish will get places. Get ready and I'll send you off."

"There's Gerald," said Alf, pointing to a youngster who, in a modest attire of sleeveless shirt, short running trunks and spiked shoes, was stepping eagerly about at a little distance. "Looks as though he could run, doesn't he? Good muscles in those legs of his. That's what boxing does for you."

"There he goes," groaned Tom. "Honest, Dan, he thinks boxing will do anything from developing the feet to raising hair on a bald head!"

"That's all right," said Alf stoutly. "It'll develop the muscles of the legs, my friend, just about as much as any other muscles. O-oh, Gerald!"

Gerald Pennimore looked around, smiled, and waved his hand. He was a good-looking youngster of fifteen, with an eager, expressive face, a lithe body that needed development, and a coloring that was almost girlish. His eyes were very blue and his skin was fair in spite of the fact that he had tried hard all the summer to get it tanned like Dan's. What bothered him more than all else, however, was the fact that his cheeks were pink and that the least emotion made him redden up like a girl. His hair, which he kept cut as short as possible, was the color of corn tassels, but the summer had streaked it with darker tones and Gerald was hopeful that in time it would all turn to an ordinary shade of brown. Another trial that he had to endure was being thought even younger than he was. It was bad enough to be only fifteen when the fellows you most liked were from one to

Winning His "Y": A Story of School Athletics

three years older, but to have folks guess your age as fourteen was very discouraging.

"All ready!" warned Andy Ryan.

Gerald poised himself in the second line of starters and waited eagerly, impatiently for the word. Then it came and he bounded off as though the race was a quarter-mile run instead of a three-mile jaunt over a hard road and some rough hills and meadows.

"Easy, Gerald!" cautioned Dan as the runners swept by. "Get your wind. Hello, Thompson! Hello, Joe! Stick to 'em!"

"There's that chap Hiltz," said Alf. "Didn't know he had enough energy to run. By the way, we mustn't forget about the Cambridge Society election next month. You've got to beat Hiltz out, you know, if we are to get Gerald in as we promised. Hiltz and Thompson were the Third Class members of the Admission Committee last year and I suppose they'll be up for election from the Second Class this year. We must find out about that, and if Hiltz is going to try to get in again you must do a little canvassing on your own hook. We'll organize a campaign. You can beat him, though, without trying, I guess."

"We made a mistake in thinking it was Thompson who blackballed Gerald in May, didn't we?"

"Yes, I guess Thompson's a pretty square sort of chap. He and Gerald are quite thick this year."

The runners trotted out of sight around a bend of the road and the three boys perched themselves on the top rail of the fence and, with the others, waited for the runners to return. Cross-country running was something new at Yardley. The sport had been growing in popularity among the colleges and from them was spreading to the preparatory schools. Broadwood, Yardley's chief rival, had sent a challenge in September and it had been accepted. Since then the school had been quite mad on the subject of cross-country running, and Andy Ryan, in the interims of his work with the football players, had been busy training candidates for a cross-country team to meet Broadwood. The dual meet was to take place on the morning of November 21st, on the afternoon of which day Yardley and

Broadwood would clash in the final football game at Broadwood, some four miles distant. Each team was to consist of ten runners, and to-day's try-out was to enable the trainer to select a dozen of the numerous candidates, two of them to be substitutes. The newly formed team was to elect a captain that evening.

Cross-country running, however, didn't long engage the attention of the three on the fence. The conversation soon turned to football, which, since they were all players, was only natural. They discussed that afternoon's game with St. John's Academy, which, although of minor importance and not difficult, was the last of the preliminary contests and would settle the fate of more than one player.

"Don't forget, fellows, that I want to stop and see Payson on the way back," said Alf. "He thinks we ought to play two twenty-minute halves, but I think a twenty and a fifteen would be better. It will be fairly warm this afternoon. What do you say?"

"I don't care," answered Tom indifferently. "Let's play what they want to play."

"It isn't up to them," said Alf. "We fix the length of halves. It's all well enough for you, Tom; you're a regular ox for work; but some of the new chaps will feel the pace, I guess."

"How long will the halves be next week with Carrel's?" asked Dan.

"Twenty, I suppose. We don't usually play twenty-fives until the Brewer game."

"Then thirty-five minutes altogether ought to be enough for to-day, I would say. Although I don't care as far as I'm concerned."

"We'll stop and talk it over with Payson," said Alf. "Did you hear that Warren, the Princeton center of last year, is going to help coach at Broadwood this fall?"

"No, really?" asked Dan.

"That's what I heard. I wish we could get a good chap to help Payson. We ought to have some one to coach the back field on catching punts and running back; some one who could come down here after the Brewer game and put in two good hard weeks."

"How about that brother of yours?" asked Tom. Alf shrugged his shoulders.

"He won't be able to get away much. He's going to come when he can, but he knows only about line men. Considering the number of fellows we send to Yale I think they might help us out a little with the coaching."

"Have they ever been asked to?"

"Oh, a couple of years ago we tried to get them to send some one down, and they did send a chap for a week or so, but he wasn't much good; just stood around and criticized the plays we were using. What we need is some one who'll take his coat off and knock some plain horse-sense into the fellows. I think I'll talk to Payson about it and see what he thinks."

"Well, look here," said Tom. "Colton's on the Yale freshman team. Why not write to him and see what he can do?"

"Colton," answered Alf dryly, "was a great big thing when he was captain here last year, but just at present he's only one of some sixty or seventy candidates trying for a place on the freshman eleven. I guess he has all the trouble he wants. Look, isn't that one of our long-distance heroes footing it down the road there?"

"Yes," answered Dan. "Come on."

They jumped down and hurried over to the finish line.

"Here they come!" some one cried, and there was a rush for places of observation. Andy Ryan got his pencil ready and handed his stop watch to Alf.

"Take the time of the first three," he directed.

"Track! Track!" The first runner trotted down the road looking rather fagged and as the trainer set his name down he crossed the line and staggered tiredly into the arms of a friend. He was Goodyear, a Second Class fellow. Fifty yards behind three runners were fighting hard for second place. They finally finished within ten feet of each other and Ryan entered their names: Henderson, Wagner, French. Two minutes passed before the next man came into sight.

"That's young Thompson," said Alf. "He doesn't look as though the distance had troubled him much, does he? Good work, Thompson! See anything of Pennimore up the line?"

"Yes," answered Arthur Thompson as he joined them, breathing hard but seemingly quite fresh after his three-mile spin. "I passed him about a mile back. He looked pretty fit, Loring, and I guess he'll finish. I hope he does."

Four boys came down the road well bunched and there was a good-natured struggle for supremacy as they neared the waiting group. "Norcross, Maury, Felder, Garson," called Andy Ryan as they crossed the line. "Don't stand around here, byes; go home and get a shower right off."

"That's nine," said Alf. "Any more in sight? If Gerald doesn't finish one of the next three he's dished. Here's another chap now. It isn't Gerald though, is it?"

"No, that's not Gerald," said Tom. "It's—What's-his-name?—Sherwood, of your class, Dan."

"Yes, I know him. Good for you, Sher! You've got a dandy color!" Sherwood grinned as he trotted by. There was another wait and then another runner came into sight at the turn, and a second later two more, running side by side.

"Gee, that'll be a race!" exclaimed Dan. "Only two of them will get places. By Jove, fellows, one of them's Gerald. See him?"

"That's right, and the fellow with him is Hiltz." Alf chuckled. "Here's a fine chance for him to get even with Hiltz for queering him with Cambridge last spring. I wonder if he can do it."

The first of the three, glancing back, eased his pace and finished a good twenty yards ahead, very tired. Gerald Pennimore and Jake Hiltz were struggling gamely for the twelfth place in the race. As they came near Alf gave a whoop.

"Gerald's got it!" he cried. "Come on, you Geraldine! You've got him beat! Dig your spikes, boy! Don't let up!"

It was a battle royal for a dozen yards at the finish, but Gerald drew ahead steadily, turning once to look at his adversary, and crossed the line two yards to the good, Alf and Tom and Dan running out to seize him in case he fell.

But Gerald had no idea of falling. Instead he walked off the road, resisting the outstretched arms, and sat down on a rock, looking up a trifle breathlessly but quite smilingly at his solicitous friends.

"I was twelfth, wasn't I?" he gasped.

"You're the even dozen, Gerald," said Dan. "How'd you do it?"

"It wasn't hard," answered Gerald. "I could have finished ahead of that fellow Groom if I'd wanted to, but I thought I'd rather have some fun with Hiltz. He was all in long ago."

This was quite evidently so, for Hiltz was lying on his back struggling for breath, with a friend supporting his head.

"Gerald," said Alf sorrowfully, "I'm afraid that's not a Christian spirit. You should—er—love your enemy."

"Oh, I love him better now," laughed Gerald, holding out his hand to be helped up. "I guess I've got even with him for keeping me out of Cambridge last year, haven't I?"

"You have," said Tom. "Get your bath robe and come on home. You fellows trot along and see Payson, if you want to; I'll go back with the kid."

CHAPTER II
HILTZ ENTERS A PROTEST

When they had crossed the bridge the four talked a while of the comet and then Dan and Alf turned to the right toward the little buff house wherein Payson, the football coach, had his lodgings, and Tom and Gerald kept on in the direction of the school. Ahead of them was a straggling line of fellows whose eager voices reached them crisply on the morning air.

"Aren't you tired?" asked Tom with a solicitous glance at the younger boy. Gerald shook his head.

"Not a bit, Tom. You see, I've been at it ever since school opened. It's wonderful the way practice brings you along. Why, when I started out I used to lose my breath in the first mile! Now I think I could run six miles and not get much winded. And you ought to see how my chest is expanding!"

"If Alf were here," laughed Tom, "he'd tell you that was due to boxing!"

"I dare say some of it is," responded Gerald smilingly. "I hope Andy will let me in the run with Broadwood. I suppose he will give us a lot of stiff work before that, though. Are you going to play this afternoon, Tom?"

"Yes. Alf's gone to see Payson about the length of halves. Payson wants two twenties and Alf thinks that's too much."

"I wish Bendix would let me play," sighed Gerald. "Don't you think it's mean of him, Tom? He says I'm not strong enough, but I'll wager I'm as strong as lots of the fellows on the Second."

"No, you're not, kid. You wait until next year. Muscles knows what he's talking about. Football's a tough game to play and a fellow needs to be pretty sturdy if he isn't going to get banged up. I like the game mighty well, but if I had a kid of my own I don't believe I'd let him look at a football before he was eighteen."

"Gee, I'd hate to be your kid!" Gerald laughed. "Think of the fun he'd miss! I'm going to play next fall, all right. Dad doesn't like it, but he's pretty fussy about me."

"Why shouldn't he be?" asked Tom. "You're the only one he's got, aren't you? If you get killed who's going to be the next Steamship King?"

"I'd rather be a lawyer," said Gerald thoughtfully.

"Well, you'll have enough money to be what you like, I guess. It won't matter whether you get a case or not."

"Dad doesn't want me to be that, though," answered Gerald as they climbed the fence and set off up the well-worn path across the meadow slope. "He says I ought to study law but he wants me to go into his office when I finish college."

"You ought to be glad you've got a fine big business all ready and waiting," said Tom. "By the way, where is that father of yours now, Gerald? I haven't seen him lately, have I?"

"He's out West; Chicago, to-day, I think. He's coming back the middle of next week. You and Alf and Dan are to take dinner with us some night after he comes home."

"Glad to." Tom unconsciously looked back across the village to where the stone gables and turrets of Sound View, the summer home of the millionaire Steamship King, arose above the trees. "How long are you going to keep the house open this fall, Gerald?" he asked.

"Until after Thanksgiving, I suppose. Dad will be away a good deal, though. You know he's combining a lot of steamship lines on the Lakes. It's keeping him pretty busy."

"I should think it might," said Tom dryly. "I guess it would be a good morning's work for me."

They climbed The Prospect, as the terrace in front of Oxford Hall is called, and parted company, Tom disappearing around the corner of the old granite building in the direction of his room in Dudley Hall and Gerald following the drive past Merle Hall to the gymnasium. The locker room was pretty well filled with boys when he entered and he fancied that the conversation, which had sounded animated enough through the folding doors, died suddenly at his appearance. He nodded to several of the fellows, among them Arthur Thompson, and crossed to his locker. From the showers came the rush of water and the yelps and groans of youths undergoing what in Yardley parlance was known as the Third Degree. The chatter began again as Gerald slipped out of his running costume and, wrapping his big Turkish towel about him, sought the baths. They were all occupied, however, and he turned back to wait his turn. Arthur Thompson was dressing a few feet away and Gerald seated himself beside him on the bench.

"I'd punch Hiltz's head," Thompson growled under his breath.

"What for?" asked Gerald.

"What for! Haven't you heard what he's saying?"

Gerald shook his head.

"No. What's he saying, Arthur?"

"Why, that you cut the course coming back. He's told Andy Ryan and about everyone else. He wants you disqualified. That would give him a place on the team, you see. I thought you'd heard it."

"Do the fellows believe it?" asked Gerald. His voice shook a little and he felt the blood dyeing his cheeks.

"I don't know," answered Arthur in a low voice. "I don't. Jake Hiltz always was a liar. I wouldn't believe him if he told me his own name!"

"Is he here?"

"Somewhere; in the shower, I guess. What are you going to do, Gerald?"

"I'm going to make him say it to me," answered Gerald hotly.

"Well, don't have any fuss with him," Arthur advised. "He's bigger than you and a couple of years older."

"I don't care how big he is. If he says I cheated, he lies!"

Gerald had unconsciously raised his voice and a big, ungainly looking youth, who at that moment emerged from one of the showers, heard and turned toward them.

"Who lies, Pennimore?" he demanded threateningly.

"You do if you say I cheated this morning, Hiltz!"

"You look out, Money-bags, or you'll get something you won't like," threatened Hiltz.

"Then you take that back," said Gerald shrilly.

"Take back nothing! I said you cut the course, and you did, and you know you did. You gained at least twenty yards on me. If it wasn't for that I'd have beaten you easily."

"That's a lie!"

Hiltz stepped forward and aimed a blow at Gerald, but Arthur Thompson caught the older boy's fist on his arm.

"Cut it out, Hiltz," he growled. "He's only half your size."

"He called me a liar!"

"Well, what of it? I wouldn't believe you on oath, Hiltz. I don't believe he cut the course."

"Nobody cares what you believe," answered Hiltz savagely. "I've put it up to Ryan and Mr. Bendix and they'll settle it without your help, my fresh friend."

"Where did I cut the course?" Gerald demanded.

"You know well enough," responded Hiltz. "At the first turn going into Greenburg. You cut across the field when you ought to have kept to the road."

"I didn't! Groom can prove it. He was right ahead all the time. Did I, Groom?"

"I don't know," answered that youth from the other end of the room. "I wasn't looking." Evidently he didn't want to be drawn into the discussion.

"Well, I didn't," reiterated Gerald. "I was right beside you all the last two miles, Hiltz, and you know it very well."

"I've said what I know. We'll see whether you can cheat me out of my place on the team. If you weren't so small I'd give you a mighty good licking for talking like that to me."

"Never mind my size," cried Gerald, rushing past Arthur. "I'm not afraid of you! I said you lied, and I say it again!"

"Cut that out, Pennimore!" interrupted a big chap who had entered. He was Durfee, a First Class fellow, and captain of the Baseball Team. "You're not big enough to fight Hiltz, so don't call him names. What's the row, anyway?"

"He says I cheated!" cried Gerald, almost on the verge of tears. "He's told Ryan that I cut the course! He's told everyone."

"Well, did you?"

"No!"

"All right; let it go at that. He says you did, you say you didn't. Your word's as good as his, I suppose. Let Ryan settle it. Move along, Jake, you're blocking the traffic."

"I'm perfectly willing to let Ryan settle it," said Hiltz, as he drew away. "But I'm not going to have that little bug call me names."

"Oh, tut, tut!" said Durfee, shoving him playfully away. "It's a pity about you, Jake. Run along now. As for you, Pennimore, just remember that it isn't good form to call names, especially to upper classmen. Besides which," he added with a smile, "it isn't wise."

"I'm not afraid of him," said Gerald. Durfee grinned and winked at Arthur Thompson.

"I wouldn't be either," he muttered as he turned away.

"You'd better see Ryan as soon as you can and tell him your side of it," Arthur advised. "I'm pretty sure Hiltz made it up because you beat him out at the finish."

"Groom knows I didn't cheat," said Gerald aggrievedly. "He just doesn't want to say so."

"Groom is all for the peaceful life," answered Arthur. "Maybe, though, Bendix will get him to fess up."

"If he doesn't, how can I prove that Hiltz isn't right?"

"You can't, I suppose. And Hiltz can't prove that you're not right. So there you are. Run along and get your shower. I'll wait for you and we'll find Andy."

The little trainer wasn't far to seek when Gerald had dressed himself. He was in the office upstairs. Arthur stayed outside while Gerald stated his case.

"And you kept to the road, you say?" asked the trainer.

"Yes, I did, Andy; and Groom knows it, only he won't say so."

"Well, I'll see him. Don't you bother; it'll be all right; be aisy in your mind, me bye."

"Shall I see Mr. Bendix?" Gerald asked.

"No, no, I'll tell him all about it. Maybe he won't have anything to do with it anyway. Sure, I don't see why I can't settle the trouble meself!"

Gerald joined Arthur and they made their way across the Yard together. As they approached the back of Whitson Hall a boy at an open window in the second story hailed them.

"Hello, Gerald! Come on up. Say, Arthur, I want you to help me with this history stuff. Will you?"

"That's what comes of having a kid for a roommate," sighed Arthur. "He doesn't try to learn anything. All he thinks of is his beastly stamp book. He's driving me crazy, talking about 'issues' and 'perforations,' and all the rest of the truck."

"Are you coming right up?" called the boy.

"Yes, I am, and when I do I'll wring your young neck," answered Arthur savagely. "Why don't you study once in a while?"

"How's the stamp collection getting on, Harry?" asked Gerald.

"Fine!" replied Harry Merrow. "I got some dandies the other day. Traded for them with 'Tiger' Smith. Come up and see them."

"Some other time, Harry. You're going to study now, you know." Harry Merrow made a face.

"What's the good of studying?" he demanded pertly. "Arthur always help me out."

"Well, he's going to stop it right now!" declared Arthur. "And, what's more, I'm going to pitch that stamp book out of the window if you don't forget it for a while. See you later, Gerald. Don't you worry about that; it'll be all right. Everyone knows Jake Hiltz."

Arthur ran up the steps and disappeared into Whitson Hall and Gerald went on to the next dormitory, Clarke, and climbed two well-worn flights of stairs. The last door in the corridor bore the number 28 and two visiting cards tacked beneath it. On one was "Daniel Morse Vinton," and on the other "Gerald Pennimore," but it was much too dark to read them. Gerald opened the door and passed through. At the end of the room, on the window seat, Dan and Alf were lolling.

"Hello," said Alf. "Behold the fleet-footed Mercury!"

"Fleet-footed perhaps," said Dan, "but not glad-visaged. What's the matter, Gerald? Anyone dead?"

"Matter enough," answered Gerald, as he tossed his cap onto the table and threw himself into the Morris chair. "Jake Hiltz has told everyone that I cut the course this morning. He's told Ryan and wants him to disqualify me."

"Phew!" whistled Dan.

"Oh, Hiltz!" said Alf contemptuously. "Don't let that worry you, kid. Hiltz couldn't tell the truth if he was paid double."

"And Groom was just ahead of us all the time, and he knows I didn't cut and he won't say so," wailed Gerald.

"Groom never says anything if he can help it," responded Alf. "Andy will fix it all right; he's nobody's fool. And he knows Jake, too. Has he got any—er—foundation for his malicious libel, Gerald? Did you wander away from the beaten path, my boy?"

"Not once," replied Gerald indignantly.

"Well, I didn't suppose you had, unless by accident," said Alf soothingly. "I suppose Jake got mad because you beat him at the finish and made up the yarn out of whole cloth. I wouldn't pay any attention to it, Gerald."

"But it's all over school!"

"Never mind. Your word is as good as Jake's; better, for that matter; fellows will know what to believe. Did you—er—encounter the gentleman?"

"Yes, he was in the gym. I told him he was a liar."

"The dickens you did! And what did he say?"

"Oh, I don't know. He tried to hit me, but Arthur Thompson got in the way, and after that Durfee came along."

"Durfee always was a kill-sport," grieved Alf.

"Shut up, Alf," said Dan. "Gerald hadn't any business getting fresh."

"Well, why did he lie about me, then?" Gerald demanded.

"When you've been in school longer, Gerald, you'll learn that you've got to put up with a lot of lies. Lies don't hurt any—as long as they *are* lies."

"Well, I wasn't afraid of him, and if——"

"You'd have gone and had a mix-up in the gym and got into a lot of trouble," interrupted Dan severely. "It's a good thing Thompson or Durfee, or whoever it was, interfered."

"Think of Arthur Thompson jumping in and saving our young hero!" chuckled Alf. "Why, last year Gerald was training to fight him to a finish. Gerald, I'll bet you could get the best of Jake Hiltz; he doesn't know a thing about boxing."

"Well, Gerald isn't going to fight Hiltz," said Dan warmly. "And I wish you'd quit putting fool ideas into his head, Alf."

"Yes, mamma! Thank you, mamma. I consider myself reproved and slapped twice on the wrist. Come on to dinner and stop worrying, Gerald. It'll all come out in the wash. And Dan's right, too. After you've been here a little longer you'll find that a fellow's got to put up with a lot of fool yarns. Just as long as you play fair you don't have to worry about what fellows say. Come on now; this is roast-beef day, and I'm as hungry as a bear!"

CHAPTER III
WHICH MAY BE SKIPPED

Yardley Hall School is at Wissining, Conn., and Wissining—for it is no use looking at your map unless it is a very detailed one—is on Long Island Sound, about halfway between New Haven and Newport. It may be that you know all about Yardley, in which case this chapter is not for you, and you have only to pass it over, and no hard feelings. I might take it for granted that everyone knows Yardley, just as they know Exeter and Andover and Groton and St. Mark's and Lawrenceville and Hillton and a dozen more. But if I did I'd probably hear from it, for there is always some one who "doesn't know." I once heard a middle-aged gentleman, who sat across from me in the parlor car, remark as the train stopped at New Haven: "New Haven? There's some sort of an educational establishment for boys here, isn't there?" So, perhaps, there are those who, when the train runs through Wissining, observe the cluster of buildings on the hilltop without knowing that they are looking at Yardley Hall School.

Yardley is not very old, as New England schools go, having been established no longer ago than 1870. It was Oxford School for Young Gentlemen in those days, and the buildings were but two in number. The founder and head master, Dr. Tobias Hewitt, an Englishman and a graduate of Oxford University, managed for a quarter of a century to conduct the school with credit and pecuniary success. Then for some reason the enrollment dwindled and the institution, which by this time boasted four buildings, passed into the hands of a stock company. Then came changes. Oxford School became Yardley Hall School, the forms became classes, the masters instructors. More buildings were erected and a great deal of money spent. Doctor Hewitt retained an interest and remained Principal. Nowadays Yardley is one of the finest preparatory schools in the country. If you doubt my word you have only to ask a Yardley student or graduate. The property comprises some forty acres of hill and meadow and woodland that runs from the shore of the sound back a good three quarters of a mile to the Wissining River, that little sluggish inconsequent stream that divides Wissining from her more citified neighbor, Greenburg.

There are four dormitories, Whitson, Clarke, Dudley, and Merle, Oxford Hall, containing the offices, the Principal's apartments, recitation rooms, laboratories, library, assembly hall and society headquarters, and the Kingdon Gymnasium, one of the best appointed in the land. These buildings, with the exception of Dudley, describe roughly a half circle around the face of the hill, with Oxford, the oldest and least attractive, in the center. In front of Oxford is a terrace called The Prospect, from which a wide view of sea and land may be had. Dudley Hall, the senior dormitory, is more retiring and stands back from the other buildings, across the Yard. Southward the ground slopes abruptly to the railroad cut, through which the main-line trains dash and long freights crawl day and night. There is a rustic bridge here, and if you keep on the paths lead you through a dense, well-kept woods to the beach and the sound. Northward the land slopes more gradually to the river and the tennis courts, athletic field and boathouse. Eastward lies the golf links with its puzzling nine-hole course. The river twists and winds north-eastward, and divides to make room for two tiny islands. Across the stream lies Meeker's Marsh, with Marsh Lake hidden behind alder and swamp willow and rushes. Here is the home of plover and snipe and duck, and, truth compels me to add, mosquitoes.

There are five classes at Yardley: Preparatory, Fourth, Third, Second, and First. The Preparatory Class fellows room in Merle, under the matronly care of Mrs. Ponder, popularly known as "Emily," and allude to themselves as "preps." First Class men call themselves seniors, and, with the Second Class, constitute the Upper Classmen. There are some two hundred and seventy students in Yardley, their ages ranging from twelve to twenty. Yardley sends most of her product to Yale, while Broadwood Academy, her dearest foe, supplies each year a fair proportion of the entering class at Princeton. Broadwood is situated some three miles inland from Greenburg, and at Yardley they like to speak of it maliciously as a "fresh-water school." Yardley and Broadwood are old-time rivals, meeting each year on the gridiron, diamond, track, and rink. For the glory of

Winning His "Y": A Story of School Athletics

Yardley let me say that the Dark Blue has triumphed more often than the green of Broadwood, although there are pages of history relating to dual contest which Yardley fellows skim hurriedly.

CHAPTER IV
POETRY AND POLITICS

"I've got that other verse," announced Dan, tossing his pencil aside and leaning back in his chair.

"I wondered what awful deed you were doing," said Alf. "Let's hear it."

They were in 7 Dudley, a cozy, comfortable room on the first floor of the dormitory. The hosts, Alf and Tom, were stretched out on the window seat, their legs apparently inextricably mixed. Dan was seated at the table where, for the past ten minutes, he had been scribbling and erasing. Supper had been over for an hour and they had discussed the events of the day to their hearts' content. The football game with St. John's had been played and won in two fifteen-minute halves and each of the three was comfortably weary and happy. The contest had not been a hard one, but the weather had been warm and, to use Tom's expression, had "taken the starch out of a fellow." The score, 11 to 0, wasn't anything to boast of, and there had been discouraging features, but it was over with now and there was no more practice until Monday afternoon and this was no time to worry. Tom stretched his arms with a sigh of lazy contentment, kicked Alf in the shins, apologized sleepily and waited for Dan to read his effusion. Dan held the sheet to the light, frowned and hesitated.

"I don't believe it's quite as good as the other one," he said apologetically.

"Who said the other was good?" asked Alf.

"You did."

"Shut up and let him read it," growled Tom. "Go ahead, Dan."

"We-ell, here it is:

"'All together! Cheer on cheer!
Victory is ours to-day!
Raise your voices loud and clear!
Yardley pluck has won the fray!

> See, the vanquished foeman quails,
> All his vaunted courage fails!
> Flaunt the blue that never pales,
>   Fighting for old Yardley!'"

"That's all right," said Tom. "What's the matter with it?"

"What are foeman quails?" asked Alf. "Besides, the plural of quail is quail and not quails."

"Go to thunder!"

"And there's another thing, Dan. I don't just like that line about lifting our voices. It suggests exertion. Now, I might lift my voice without much trouble, but just imagine Tom trying to lift that heavy croak of his! He'd break his back at it! Why don't you — —"

"You're an idiot," said Dan good-naturedly.

"Let's sing it," suggested Alf. "How's the tune go? That's it! All together, now!"

They sang it several times, until they had learned the words, much to the distress of neighbors who protested with groans and howls. Then they sang both verses.

"That's a mighty good song," announced Tom at last, pausing for breath. "It's better than anything we've had. You ought to get somebody to write down the tune, though, before Alf changes it entirely. Can you do it, Dan?"

"No, I wish I could."

"Take it to Paul Rand," said Alf. "He's a regular dabster at music. The only criticism I have to make, Dan, is that your verses lack ginger. You've got some awfully fine words in them, but they're — well, sort of flabby. I'll bet I could write a verse to that song that would wake you up a bit. Who's got a pencil?"

He sat up and disentangled his legs.

"Lie down," protested Tom. "Hide the pencils, Dan."

But Alf went over to the table and dumped Dan out of his seat.

"Everyone very quiet now, please, while the muse gets busy. I feel the spell coming on."

Dan retired to the window seat, where he and Tom uttered gibes while Alf's pencil scratched on the paper.

"Doesn't he remind you of Tennyson—not?" inquired Tom.

"Looks to me more like Milton," Dan opined thoughtfully.

"I'll bet that was a dandy line! Alf, you aren't holding your mouth quite right. A little more curl on the left, please."

"Bright and sparkling, showing the teeth," advised Dan.

But Alf wrote on, supremely indifferent to interruptions, and at last dropped his pencil with a smile of triumph.

"Just you listen to this!" he cried.

"Go head," said Tom, "but please wave your hand when you come to a rhyme so we'll know it."

"Subside, brute! Listen:

> "'Yell like thunder! Cheer on cheer!
>   Kill the enemy quite dead!
> Punch his nose and bite his ear,
>   Kick him on his little head!
> We will give old Broadwood fits,
>   Frighten her out of her wits!
> We will chew her all to bits,
>   Fighting for old Yardley!'"

"Now, that's something like, isn't it? Has go and ginger to it, what?"

"Wonderful!" laughed Dan. "Such pretty thoughts!"

"Just full of quaint and cheerful sentiments!" said Tom. "Sounds like an automobile accident."

"We'll have that for the third verse," said Alf, grinning. "But I must have credit for it. 'First two verses by Dan Vinton; last verse by Alf Loring; all rights reserved.'"

24

"'Copyrighted in New Jersey and all foreign countries,'" added Dan. "Why don't you send that to the *Scholiast*, Alf. It's better than most of the poetry they print."

"Well, I think myself," responded Alf modestly, "that it has more feeling and delicacy. Say, where's Little Geraldine to-night?"

"With Arthur Thompson, I guess," answered Dan. "They're getting pretty thick these days."

"You guess!" said Alf severely. "What sort of a guardian are you, I'd like to know. What do you suppose John T. Pennimore would say if he knew that you had let the child out of your sight without being certain where he is?"

"Is he still worried about this morning?" asked Tom.

"I think so, but I tell him that no one will believe Hiltz."

"By the way," said Alf, squeezing himself onto the seat between them, "I've found out that Hiltz is expecting to get on the Second Class Admission Committee again, he and Thompson both. Of course we don't have to worry about Thompson, but if we want to get Gerald into Cambridge this year it's up to you, Dan, to beat Hiltz out for the committee."

"What'll I have to do?"

"Just let the fellows in the Second know that you're after the place, that's all. It's simple enough, and you ought not have much trouble beating Jake Hiltz. If you don't, though, he will blackball Gerald as sure as anything, especially after what happened to-day, and, as you know, one blackball will keep him out. And after that there's nothing left for him but an ignominious admission to Oxford."

Tom, the only Oxford Society man of the three, grunted sarcastically.

"All right," Dan agreed. "I'll start my campaign. I suppose the thing to do is to see all the fellows I know and get them to promise to vote for me. When does the election come off?"

"Well, the classes elect committee members about the first of November; I don't know just what the date is, but we can find out. Then the society election comes off the first Wednesday after the second Monday in the new moon, or something idiotic like that; anyhow, it's about the twenty-third of November. Let's go over to Cambridge and find out all about it. Besides, there'll be a lot of fellows there and you can get in your work."

"All right. Better come along, Tom."

"I'm particular where I go," muttered Tom sleepily. Alf threw a book at him playfully and escaped before Tom could make reprisal.

Secret societies are tabooed at Yardley, although now and again one gets hints of mysterious meetings behind draped transoms at dead o' night. But both faculty and undergraduate sentiment is opposed to such things and they soon die of inanition. The two recognized societies are Cambridge and Oxford. They are both debating clubs, although of recent years they have become rather more social than anything else. At one time or another every student has the opportunity to join one or other of the societies, but to be invited to each is considered something of an honor. This had happened to Gerald Pennimore the preceding spring, when Alf and Dan had tried to get him into Cambridge, and Tom, supported by a handful of influential friends, had offered Gerald the hospitality of Oxford. Gerald had chosen Cambridge, but thanks to Jacob Hiltz, then one of the two Third Class members of the Admission Committee, he had received one blackball, sufficient to bar him out. Dan and Alf had thereupon made up their minds to secure Gerald's election this fall, and in order to do that it was necessary to defeat Hiltz for the Admission Committee, and Dan had agreed to run against him.

The rooms of the rival societies were on the top floor of Oxford Hall. Each was large and comfortably furnished, with plenty of cushioned window seats and easy chairs, tables for writing and good reference libraries. Many fellows made use of the rooms during the day to study in between recitations, while in the evenings they were pretty certain to be well filled with members reading or playing chess, checkers, dominoes, or cards. To-night, when Dan and Alf entered Cambridge, the weekly debate had just been finished and the thirty or forty fellows present were moving their chairs back against the walls, preparatory to social diversions. A few minutes later they had formed a group in a corner of the room with Paul Rand and Joe Chambers. Both were seniors and prominent in Cambridge affairs,

Chambers being president and Rand secretary. Chambers was editor-in-chief of the school weekly, the *Scholiast*, while Rand was manager of the basket-ball team. Chambers soon supplied the information they desired as to election dates.

"Dan's a candidate for the Second Class Admission Committee," explained Alf. "By the way, who are the members in your class, Paul?"

"Derrick and I," answered Rand.

"That's all right, then. We want to get young Pennimore in next month. You haven't anything against him, I suppose?"

"Not a thing."

"And how about you, Joe?"

"Same here," replied Chambers. He was a tall, intellectual-looking youth who wore glasses and was popularly believed to be an embryo great journalist.

"Good enough," said Alf. "You'd better get busy, Dan, and hunt up some of your class fellows and get them pledged. There's Walpole over there; tackle him."

But Walpole was very sorry and had just promised Hiltz to vote for him. "Wish I had known before, Dan," he said. "I'd rather stood for you if you'd told me. I didn't know you were running."

It didn't take Dan long to discover that Hiltz had been busy, for everyone of the dozen or so Second Classmen he spoke to had been approached by his adversary. A few only had not definitely promised their support and these willingly pledged their votes to Dan. Dan went back to the group in the corner.

"Say, Paul, how many Second Class fellows are there in Cambridge?"

"I can tell you in a minute." Rand went to his desk, unlocked a drawer and looked over the membership list. "Twenty-nine," he announced, returning with the list in his hand. "Want to get the names?"

"Yes," said Dan, "that's a bully idea. Read them out to me, will you?" So Paul read and Dan jotted them down on a piece of paper. When he had finished he said: "I've seen eleven to-night and seven of them are promised to Hiltz. If that ratio works out with the rest I'll get only about ten votes." He looked doubtfully at Alf.

"I don't believe Hiltz has seen them all," answered Alf. "What you want to do is to get busy right away. There's Thompson now. Talk to him, Dan."

Arthur Thompson had just entered with Gerald in tow and Dan crossed over to them.

"Hello, Thompson, I want to speak to you a minute. This is your first visit this year, isn't it, Gerald?"

"Yes, Arthur invited me up. Is the debate over?"

"Yes, ten minutes ago. Alf's over there in the corner, with Paul and Joe Chambers. I want to speak to Thompson just a second."

Gerald wandered away toward the group and Dan plunged into his subject.

"I say, Thompson, you're up for Admission Committee, aren't you?"

"Yes."

"Well, I suppose you don't vote for yourself, do you?"

"Hardly," laughed Arthur. "It's customary to vote for the other candidate and he votes for you. It amounts to the same thing, I suppose."

"Any objection to voting for me?"

"You? You're not up, are you?"

"Yes, and I'm up to beat Jake Hiltz. We want to get Gerald through this time and Hiltz will down him as sure as fate. He did last spring, you know, and he's bound to now after what happened this morning."

"That's so. All right, I'll vote for you, Vinton. But I'm mighty afraid that Hiltz has the thing cinched. I'd withdraw and give you my votes, but that wouldn't defeat Hiltz. I wish it would. But I'll help you all I can."

"Will you? Then just look at this list and see what fellows you think you can influence."

Arthur looked it over. Then he took out his pen and copied half a dozen of the names on the back of an envelope. "I'll look after these," he said in a businesslike way, "the first thing in the morning. Is Jake here to-night?"

"He was before the debate, but he's gone. Maybe he's canvassing now. I wonder— —"

"What?"

"I wonder why he's so anxious to be reëlected, Thompson."

"That's so! He hasn't said a thing about it to me. It looks as though he had just started in to-day, doesn't it? Do you suppose— —"

"That he wants to get back so as to defeat Gerald again? I wouldn't be a bit surprised. It certainly looks that way. I've spoken to eleven fellows here this evening and they all said that Hiltz had been after them before the debate."

"Then that's just what he's up to, Vinton! You heard about the protest he made against Gerald?"

"Yes; just one of his lies, of course."

"Yes, Gerald doesn't cheat. And I guess he knows that Ryan isn't likely to believe him and thinks he will get revenge in this way. Well, we'll do our best to beat him, Vinton. But we've got to look sharp. He's pretty foxy, Jake is."

"And he's got seven fellows pledged to him already," said Dan frowningly.

"How about you?" asked Arthur.

"Five, counting you."

"That's not so bad! I'll come around to-morrow after I've seen some of these chaps and let you know what I've done. You'll have to have fifteen votes, won't you? Well, there's three on this list that I'm sure you can count on, and that makes eight. And if Jake hasn't got ahead of us the other seven won't be hard to find."

"No, but I'm awfully afraid he has," said Dan gloomily.

"We'll know in the morning," answered Arthur cheerfully. "I'll drop around to your room in the afternoon, probably. So long."

CHAPTER V
DAN BUYS A TICKET

The next day was Sunday and there was church in the village in the forenoon and a big dinner afterwards, and at two o'clock Dan and Gerald were sprawled out in 28 Clarke, making a not very convincing pretense at studying when Arthur Thompson called. He glanced doubtfully at Gerald as he found a seat.

"Want him to hear?" he asked. Dan nodded.

"It doesn't matter, I guess. What luck did you have?"

Thompson drew a list from his pocket and tossed it over.

"The ones with crosses opposite are sure," he explained, "and those with circles are doubtful. The rest are promised to Jake."

"I don't mind going out, if you like," said Gerald.

"Not a bit of it," answered Dan. "Stay where you are. It's only about the election of the Second Class Admission Committee. I've decided to run with Thompson, that's all." He studied the list in his hand.

"Well, you did better than I did, Thompson," he said finally. "I saw six fellows before church and got only two. You've got three."

"And two doubtful."

"How doubtful?"

"Well, Murdock says he has half promised but will vote for you if Jake will let him off, and Simms said he doesn't care who's elected, but thinks Jake ought to have it again if he wants it. I told him you were the better man of the two and he said he guessed that was so and would think it over."

Dan shrugged his shoulders.

"Simms doesn't like me and you can count him out. Well, I've still got three fellows to see; couldn't find them this morning. One of them, Brewster, has gone home; has quinsy or tonsilitis or something."

"So I heard. He will be back this week, though, I guess. And the election is two weeks away. Maybe we can find the rest of the votes in that time. How many more do we need, Vinton?"

"Five; we've got ten and have to have fifteen."

"I think you can count on Murdock, and that makes eleven."

"That leaves four and only three fellows to get them from. Some one will have to vote twice." Dan smiled as he handed back the list.

"Who are the two besides Brewster?" Arthur asked.

"Hammel and Lowd."

Arthur shook his head. "Hammel may be all right; I don't know much about him; but Caspar Lowd is a particular friend of Hiltz."

"He isn't now," said Gerald, looking up from his book. "They had some sort of a row last spring."

"That so? Well, if you can get those two, Vinton, you'll be short only one vote; and that may just come by accident; or some fellow may change his mind before election."

"I guess that's the only hope," said Dan. "Do you know Brewster?"

"Only to speak to."

"That's about the limit of my acquaintance. But I guess it doesn't matter. I'm going to get his home address from the office and write to him this evening."

"That's a good scheme. And I wouldn't wait too long, for Jake may think of the same thing. As the motto says, 'Do it now!'"

"I will." Dan laid his book down, pulled himself out of his chair and reached for his cap. "Want to walk over that way? I'll be back in a minute, chum."

Gerald nodded and Dan and Arthur went out and made their way across to Oxford. They found Mr. Forisher, the secretary, at his desk and Dan made his request. The secretary laid his pen down and swung around in his swivel chair to the card catalogue behind him.

"Brewster must be getting very popular," he remarked dryly. "This is the second time within an hour I've been asked for his address." Dan and Arthur exchanged glances.

"Who asked before, sir?" Dan questioned. "Was it Hiltz?"

"Hiltz, yes. Well, the address is— Here, I'll write it down for you." He did so and Dan took it, thanked him and hurried out.

"When does the first mail go East, Arthur?" he asked.

"I don't know, but I guess on the afternoon train. If you write that now and take it down to the station and post it on the train— —"

"Just what I mean to do. No use going to the room; I'll write it in the library. Come on."

The library was deserted, save for two preparatory youngsters who were whispering and giggling together in a corner and an older boy who was seated at one of the broad tables writing. Arthur pressed Dan's arm.

"There he is now," he whispered. Hiltz hadn't heard or seen them and they retreated quickly and noiselessly.

"He's writing to Brewster this minute," murmured Arthur, when they were back in the dim corridor. "You run over to my room and write the letter and I'll stay here and see what Jake does with his. If he posts it in the box at the door you'll have half a day on him, for they don't collect from there until six to-night."

"All right," answered Dan. "Got paper and envelopes there?"

"In the left-hand drawer. Merrow's there; make him show you."

Dan hurried off to Arthur's room in Whitson. Harry Merrow was not in, but he had no trouble finding writing materials and soon had his brief letter written. As he returned around the corner of Oxford Arthur and Jake Hiltz sauntered out of the building together and Hiltz crossed the steps, raised the lid of the letter box and deposited his letter. Dan smiled. The two came down the steps and Dan nodded as he reached them.

"Hello, Hiltz," he said. "Hello, Thompson."

Hiltz returned his greeting affably, for he liked to stand in with the fellows of prominence, and Thompson asked Dan where he was going.

"Just for a walk. Want to come along?"

"Yes, if you don't go too fast. I ate too much dinner. So long, Jake."

Hiltz had evidently intended joining them, but Arthur's dismissal changed his mind. "So long," he muttered.

Dan and Arthur descended The Prospect and when out of earshot Dan asked:

"Did you see the letter?"

"Yep; it was for Brewster all right."

"Then this is where we get ahead of him," chuckled Dan. "What time does that train go through?"

"About a quarter past three, I think. By Jove, though!"

"What?"

"We're a couple of idiots! It doesn't stop unless there's some one to get off or on! I'd forgotten that."

"So had I," answered Dan glumly. "When's the next one?"

"Not until evening, I guess, and that's the one Jake's letter will go on. Smart, aren't we?"

"Got any money on you?"

"About a dollar; why?"

"Lend it to me until we get back, will you?"

"Of course, but what are you going to do?"

"Buy a ticket to New York," answered Dan grimly.

"To New York! But you don't want to go to New York!"

"I want to stop that train, though. I'll buy a ticket and they'll flag the train. You take the letter and post it in the slot on the mail car. Then I'll decide to postpone my trip." Dan laughed at Arthur's expression of admiring awe.

"You're a wonder! I'd never have thought of that! But won't they be peeved?"

"Let them. I've got a perfect right to buy a ticket and have the train stopped. If I change my mind about going at the last minute it's no one's business but mine. What time is it, I wonder." He glanced at his watch. "Let's hit it up a bit, Thompson. I'd hate to lose the train!"

Thompson laughed enjoyably. "Gee, I wouldn't have missed this for a farm!" he said. "Can't you just see the conductor's face when you don't get on the train?"

The little station was empty when they reached it save for the presence of the agent who, tilted back in his chair at the telegraph desk at the open window, was yawning behind his Sunday newspaper.

"Does the express that comes along about three-fifteen stop here?" asked Dan.

"No," replied the agent, glancing up briefly, "not unless there's some one to get on or off."

"That's all right, then. I'd like a ticket for New York, please." The agent glanced at the clock and laid down his paper. It almost exhausted the combined resources of the two boys to pay for the ticket, but they managed it and had a little to spare.

"Any baggage?" asked the agent. Dan told him no, and they followed him out and watched him set the signal. The next moment the train whistled across the river at Greenburg and when the agent came back along the platform Dan and Arthur were bidding each other an affecting and almost tearful good-by.

"You drop me a line, Thompson," begged Dan, "and tell me how everything's going. Take good care of Jake and the faculty, won't you? And see that Kilts wears his goloshes when it's damp."

"Look after yourself, Vinton," begged Arthur. "You'd better wire me from the city, so I'll know you're all right and won't worry."

"I will. Good-by!"

"Good-by, old man, good-by. Do be careful of yourself and watch out for automobiles at the crossings."

"I will. And you be good to the faculty while I'm gone. See that Noah gets his warm milk every morning. My love to Old Toby. Good-by!"

"Good-by, Vinton." They wrung each other's hands and dashed a few unmanly tears from their eyes as the big locomotive charged clanging down upon them with brakes set and rasping. Arthur hurried after it up the platform with the letter in his hand. The vestibule doors swung open and the porters leaned inquiringly out as the train stopped.

"Express for New Haven, Bridgeport, Stamford, and New York!" called the conductor. "All aboard!"

Dan, hands in pocket, surveyed the conductor with a thoughtful frown.

"Who's going? You, sir?" The conductor glanced impatiently from the agent to Dan. The agent hurried across the platform.

"This is your train, boy! Hurry up and get on."

Dan shook his head slowly. Up the platform Arthur was sauntering back with a broad smile on his face.

"I guess I won't go, thanks," said Dan. "I've just remembered that I didn't bring my pyjamas."

"*What!*" The conductor glared at the agent. "What did you set that signal for?"

"He bought a ticket," answered the agent aggrievedly, "and said he wanted to go to New York."

The conductor sprang up the steps, waving his hand to the impatient engineer.

"The next time," he called crossly, "you'd better decide what you want to do! This isn't a trolley car! All right!" The vestibule doors slammed shut and in another moment the express was entering the cut, the last car flirting by in a cloud of dust with an insulted air.

Winning His "Y": A Story of School Athletics

"'I guess I won't go, thanks,' said Dan."

"You're a nice one," charged the agent. "Thought you wanted to go to New York. Want to get me in trouble, do you?"

"I do want to go to New York," answered Dan earnestly. "I'd like nothing better. But when I got to thinking it over I decided that I oughtn't to expect the school to get along without me."

"Oh, you did!" said the agent suspiciously, looking from Dan's preternaturally sober countenance to Arthur's trembling mouth. "One of your fool tricks, I suppose. I got a good mind to report this to Doctor Hewitt, I have."

"I don't see why you need be so impatient with me," complained Dan plaintively. "What difference does it make whether I got on the train or not? You ought to be glad that I've listened to the voice of duty."

"Yah!" muttered the agent, turning on his heel and retiring to the station. Dan smiled sweetly and winked at Arthur.

"Did you post it?" he asked.

"Sure!"

"Good." Dan drew his ticket to New York from a pocket and observed it reflectively. "I guess I won't want this for a while," he said. "Guess the money will be more useful." He followed the agent inside and knocked on the window.

"Well, what is it now?" inquired the official as he slammed the window up.

"I'd like to have you redeem this for me, if you please, sir," said Dan politely. The agent glared from the ticket to Dan. Then he picked it up and tossed it onto the table.

"All right. Come around in a couple of weeks and you'll get the money. But if you try any more fool tricks like this on me I'll go up to school and report you!"

Down crashed the window. Dan viewed Arthur sorrowfully and led the way out of the station. They laughed and chuckled over the episode all the way back to school, and it was only when they parted at the first entrance to Whitson that Dan's thoughts reverted to more serious matters. Then:

"I guess Hiltz doesn't know yet that I'm running against him, Thompson. He was much too pleasant to me."

"No, I'm pretty sure he doesn't. But he will find out pretty soon; some of the fellows will tell him. Then he *will* be mad!"

Winning His "Y": A Story of School Athletics

"I guess I can stand it," replied Dan philosophically. "Anyway, now that I've started this thing I'm going to see it through. And I'm going to win out if it's anyhow possible, Hiltz or no Hiltz!"

CHAPTER VI
CONDUCTING A CAMPAIGN

On Monday Andy Ryan gave his decision regarding Jake Hiltz's protest of Gerald in the cross-country trial. Both Hiltz and Gerald were to be retained on the squad.

"That," explained Andy, "will make thirteen of you instead of twelve, and it ain't likely that either of you or Hiltz will get in the race with Broadwood, but, of course, something might happen to give you a chance. So you can train with the team or not, just as you like."

"I'll keep on," said Gerald. "If I didn't fellows might think you believed Hiltz's story and had put me off."

"Well, I'm not worrying about what he said," confided Andy. "Maybe he thought you cut the corner, but——"

"He knows very well I didn't!" exclaimed Gerald indignantly.

"Well, well, it doesn't matter," said the trainer soothingly. "I'll keep you both. That gives us three substitutes, you and Hiltz and Groom. If anything happens to one of the first ten, then one of you boys will get your chance, and I'll take the one that shows up best between now and the race, no matter how you finished Saturday."

That seemed fair enough and Gerald couldn't object, although he had hoped for a vindication from the trainer. The cross-country squad went to a training table a few days later, for, although the race with Broadwood was more than a month distant, the school had set its heart on winning and Andy meant that it should. There was a run three afternoons a week for varying distances, although it was not until a week before the final contest that the team was sent over the full course. Meanwhile relations between Jake Hiltz and Gerald remained strained. It was embarrassing at first, having to sit right across the table three times a day from Hiltz, but Gerald soon got used to it. For a while Hiltz never wasted an opportunity to nag the younger boy, but the rest of the squad soon got tired of it and came to Gerald's rescue and Hiltz gave it up. Besides, he had plenty of other troubles by that time.

Winning His "Y": A Story of School Athletics

He was exceedingly angry with Dan for entering the race for committeeman, and, while he was pretty certain of reëlection, he didn't neglect any chances. He never quite understood how Dan had got ahead of him with Brewster, and when that absent youth replied to his letter by informing him that he had already pledged his vote to Vinton, Hiltz was both astounded and angry. He had always intended seeking reëlection, for the office carried not a little honor with it, but Dan and Arthur were correct in their surmise that it had been his grudge against Gerald which had set him suddenly to work securing pledges. He was quite certain that Gerald would come up again for election to Cambridge, and, since he had defeated him in the spring when his dislike to the millionaire's son had been general rather than personal, he certainly wasn't going to let him get in now when he detested him as much as he did. Besides Hiltz's dislike for Gerald there was also his dislike of Gerald's sponsors to egg him on. Hiltz envied both Dan and Alf, just as he envied any fellow who had secured honor and popularity denied him, and with Hiltz envy was akin to hate. So, in a way of speaking, he had three reasons for securing reëlection to the Admission Committee and keeping Gerald out of Cambridge.

The election of Admission Committees by the First, Second, and Third Classes was to take place on the first Wednesday in November. Meanwhile Dan and Arthur Thompson were busy. Hiltz had soon learned of Arthur's defection and had entered him in his bad books also. Murdock had finally agreed to vote for Dan. Brewster, too, was pledged, and Dan had at last persuaded Caspar Lowd to promise him his vote. Therefore, out of twenty-nine votes Dan was practically sure of thirteen, two less than necessary to secure his election.

"I know where you can get one vote," said Arthur, one day, less than a week before the election.

"Where?" asked Dan eagerly.

Arthur pointed his pencil at Dan. "Why, vote for yourself," he said. "Why not?"

"Because—" Dan hesitated. "Oh, I don't like the idea of it."

"Nonsense! You don't suppose that Jake will vote for you, do you?"

"No, not much. But, just the same— Besides, I'd still be short a vote, Arthur."

"Well, if you should find that other vote will you agree to cast your own vote where it'll do the most good?"

"I'll think it over," answered Dan. "I don't suppose there's any good reason why I shouldn't."

"Of course there isn't! It's only a matter of courtesy to vote for your opponent, and you certainly don't owe any courtesy to Jake Hiltz."

"I'll think about it; and I'll ask Alf and Tom what they think."

"All right. If only we could get Hammel to change his mind; or Simms."

"I don't want Simms's vote," said Dan.

"Oh, shucks, a vote's a vote, isn't it? Besides, you haven't anything against Simms, have you?"

"No, but I know pretty well that he doesn't like me, and so I don't want him to vote for me."

"Personal likes and dislikes," quoth Arthur oracularly, "shouldn't enter into politics."

"But I fancy they do a good deal," laughed Dan. "What time do the elections come off?"

"Three to three-fifteen in Oxford F. And we've got to do some hustling that day and see that our constituents get to the polls. Gee, if a couple of Jake's henchmen failed to show up in time to vote it would help a lot, wouldn't it? But they won't; Jake will be right after them. And so must we be. I wonder if we ought to provide carriages for our voters."

"We might get Gerald to loan us his father's automobile," laughed Dan. "It's down there at Sound View not doing a thing."

"Say, that would make a hit, wouldn't it? Maybe if we could tell some of Jake's supporters that if they voted for you they'd be taken from their rooms to Oxford in an automobile, we could land the election for you!"

"I guess that's the only way we can land it," said Dan dubiously. "I'm going to talk things over with Alf. He was cut out for a politician. Want to come along?"

"Can't; I have to study a bit. I'll look in to-morrow. There goes Gerald. I wonder if he knows what a mint of trouble you're taking to get him elected to Cambridge."

"I fancy he suspects," said Dan, with a smile. "He isn't a fool, Gerald isn't. Well, see you to-morrow then. So long, Arthur. Thanks for taking so much trouble for me. I'll try and do something for you some day to make up."

"Pshaw, you don't need to! I like it! I only hope we succeed, that's all."

They got up from where they had been sitting on the steps of Whitson and Arthur rattled upstairs to his room while Dan went across the Yard to Dudley. Alf's and Tom's room was on the ground floor and so it wasn't necessary to enter the building in order to discover whether they were at home. Dan simply put his head in at the open window.

"Anyone in?" he asked.

"No, we're both out," replied Tom, from the window seat, making a grab for Dan and just missing. Dan looked carefully about the Yard and then swung himself in through the casement, trampling on Tom and bringing a groan of protest from that recumbent youth.

"If faculty sees you do that," remonstrated Alf from the table, "you'll get fits."

"What faculty doesn't see won't hurt them," returned Dan. "What's happened to your nose, Alf?"

"Haven't you seen this before?" inquired Alf, feeling gingerly of the strip of plaster that marred the beauty of his countenance. "I got that yesterday in practice. I think Tom handed it to me, although he pretends he didn't. All I know is that he mistook me for the second once and tried to lay me out."

"Didn't," growled Tom. "You got mixed on your signals, as per usual, and got in the way."

"Isn't broken, is it?" asked Dan anxiously.

"No, just gouged out a bit, and rather swelly. What's new?"

"Nothing, I guess. But I wanted to ask you fellows something."

"You have come to the right place for knowledge," said Alf cheerfully. "We are the Oracle Brothers."

"Well, see here, would it be all right for me to vote for myself next Wednesday?"

"If you can't find a good candidate," responded Alf gravely.

"Oh, shut up! I'm in earnest. I'm short two votes as it stands now and Thompson says I ought to agree to vote for myself if we can get hold of another vote anywhere."

"Of course you ought," said Alf. "What beastly nonsense! Why not?"

"Well, it isn't done generally, is it?"

"Sometimes it isn't, but I guess that's only when the candidate is sure of his election."

"What do you think, Tom?"

"I say vote for whoever you want elected, no matter whether it's you or another chap. Your vote's as good as anyone's and you might as well have it. If I were you I'd vote for Thompson and Vinton."

"Honest?"

"Honest."

"Well, I guess I will, then—that is, if I can find the other vote. If I can't it won't matter who I vote for."

"Still shy one?" asked Alf. "Can't you induce any of Hiltz's followers to change their minds?"

"I think plenty of them would like to, but Hiltz made them promise—cross-my-heart-and-hope-to-die, you know—that they'd vote for him. Naturally they don't like to break their promises."

"Well, accidents have happened," said Alf. "Some fellow may forget to show up, or be sick, or break a leg, or something on Wednesday."

"Jake will see that none of those things happen to his voters. If any fellow breaks his leg I'll bet it will be one of mine."

"One of your legs?"

"Voters, you idiot."

"What time does the election come off?" asked Tom, laying aside his book.

"Three to three-fifteen on Wednesday, Tom."

"Polls close promptly at three-fifteen, do they?"

"I suppose so," said Dan.

"You want to insist that they shall," said Alf. "Unless, of course, one of your voters is late."

"Who are some of the fellows promised to Hiltz?" continued Tom, looking dreamily out of the window. Dan ran over a dozen of them and Tom nodded now and then.

"Look here," he said finally, "I want you to promise me something, Dan. Promise me to vote for yourself whether you get that other vote or not. Will you? You see, you can't tell until the count how many votes you've got, and you'd feel pretty sore afterwards if you discovered that you'd missed it by one vote that you might have given yourself."

"That's so, Dan," agreed Alf. "You'd better do it anyway."

"All right, I will."

"And, Dan," went on Tom sleepily as he took up his book again, "let me know Wednesday morning how things stand, will you?"

"Yes, if I don't forget."

"Just try and remember. I—I'm awfully interested in school politics and—er—elections and—" His voice died away. Dan smiled across at Alf, but Alf was regarding Tom with a puzzled, thoughtful expression on his face.

CHAPTER VII
THE ELECTION

Room F was one of the larger recitation rooms in Oxford, a rectangular, high-ceilinged apartment, with tall windows along one side and a dismal expanse of blackboard occupying most of the remaining wall space. There were some thirty seats, and a small platform at one end supported a desk and chair. On Wednesday, at a few minutes before three in the afternoon, Room F was well filled and the corridor outside was noisy with the sound of voices and the tramping of feet. The First and Third Classes were holding or were about to hold their elections in neighboring rooms, and there was quite a little excitement in the air. It was the Second Class election, however, that aroused the most interest. Usually the elections are cut-and-dried affairs, but Dan's appearance in the race had raised the contest out of the humdrum level, and even Second Class fellows who were not Cambridge members had caught the excitement and were waiting in the corridors to learn the result.

"First elects Rand and Derrick," announced Arthur Thompson, entering the room. "Isn't it time to start things here, fellows?"

"It's only two minutes of three," objected Hiltz, who was doing a little final electioneering over by the windows.

"Then your watch is slow," retorted Arthur. "First's closed her polls and counted. What time have you got, Lowd?"

"Three-four."

"Then let's get busy. Is Chambers here?"

"Here and waiting," answered Joe. "Got your slips ready?"

"They're on the desk there, aren't they? They were there when I came in."

"I've got them. Gentlemen, the polls are open. Please write the names of two candidates and your own name on the slips, fold, and then hand them to me."

Winning His "Y": A Story of School Athletics

The fellows crowded up for the slips of blank paper and then retired to the seats to prepare their ballots. Chambers took his seat at the desk and laid the roster of voters' names open in front of him. As usual pencils and pens were scarce and had to be handed around from one to another. Arthur sought Dan where the latter was filling out his ballot on a window ledge.

"Are all your fellows here, Dan?" he whispered.

"I think so. I thought I'd check them off from Chambers's list as they voted."

"I suppose that's the best. If they wouldn't keep moving around so we could check them off now. Jake was trying to get Lowd back into the fold awhile ago; did you notice? But I guess he didn't succeed, for I heard Lowd tell him to run away!"

One by one the voters handed their folded slips to Joe Chambers and gave their names. Joe laid the ballots in an open drawer at his side and crossed off the voter's name on the roster, announcing it aloud as he did so. Both Dan and Arthur got their votes in early, and Hiltz was only a minute behind them. Then the first two, who had drawn apart to watch and confer, noticed excitement in the Hiltz camp. Hiltz compared the list he held with that on the desk, searched the room with his gaze, talked vehemently with one of his supporters, and finally dispatched that youth on an errand.

"Somebody's missing," said Dan in low tones. "What time is it?"

"Ten after. They'll have to hurry if they want to get him."

Hiltz was plainly nervous and anxious, passing from the window to the door, disappearing in the corridor and hurrying back again.

"Well, our fellows are all here," said Arthur. "Murdock is voting now, and he's the last one. Look at Hiltz, will you! I'm going to see who's missing."

Arthur wormed his way through the group about the desk and leaned over the list. While he was gone a sandy-haired fellow approached Dan.

"I hope you'll win, Vinton," he said. "It was funny about that letter of yours. It came at about eleven one morning, and then at three that afternoon I got a letter from Hiltz asking me to vote for him. I was glad yours came first, though, for I'd rather you got it."

"Why, thanks, Brewster," answered Dan cordially. "That was funny, though, wasn't it? I'm glad I got there first."

"So'm I. Hope you beat him." And Brewster strolled away just as Arthur Thompson came back with his eyes dancing with excitement.

"It's that pill, Conover," he said in a low voice. "Everyone else has voted. And it's fourteen minutes past," he added, glancing at his watch. "If he doesn't come in the next minute you'll win for sure, Dan!"

"Jove!" muttered Dan, looking at his own timepiece. "Say, do you mind asking to have the polls closed as soon as time's up? It will look better coming from you."

"I'll do it, don't you worry." Arthur kept his eyes on the minute hand of his watch. Hiltz, surrounded by three or four of his friends, was talking angrily, and referring every few seconds to the watch held in his hand.

"Three-fifteen, Chambers," called Arthur, stepping up to the desk. "Let's start the count and get through. Some of the fellows have got to report for football in a few minutes."

Chambers looked at his own watch.

"All right," he said. "Has everyone here voted? Is Conover in the room?"

"He will be here in a minute," called Hiltz. "It isn't a quarter past yet."

"My watch says it is," responded Chambers mildly, "but——"

"So does mine," interrupted Arthur. "It's almost sixteen after. The polls are supposed to close at three-fifteen."

"My watch says three-thirteen," said Hiltz angrily, "and I know that it is right. Besides, if it isn't, you didn't open the polls until four minutes after three. You've got to allow fifteen minutes, Chambers."

"Well, I guess there's no objection to that, is there?" asked Chambers, glancing around.

But it seemed that there was much objection, and things began to get noisy and disputatious in Room F. And just when Chambers was insisting on silence there was a knock on the door.

"He's come!" groaned Arthur.

But when the door opened it was only the messenger that entered.

"Did you find him?" called Hiltz, hurrying across the room. "Is he coming?"

"Couldn't find him anywhere, Jake. I've been all over the school!"

Hiltz glared a moment at the boy and then turned on his heel and walked to the window, and — —

"Polls closed!" announced Chambers.

Arthur clapped Dan on the shoulder.

"You've won!" he whispered gleefully. But Dan shook his head.

"Better wait and see. You can't be sure yet."

The room quieted down while Chambers opened the ballots and tabulated the votes. It didn't take him long, and after he had been over the ballots a second time, he rapped on the desk.

"Here's the result, fellows. Quiet, please.

    THOMPSON, 26.
    VINTON, 15.
    HILTZ, 13.

"Thompson and Vinton are elected."

Pandemonium broke loose for a minute, during which Dan, striving to hide his satisfaction under a quiet smile, was congratulated by friend and foe alike. Only Hiltz kept away and, a moment later, left the room, frowning darkly, perhaps in search of the renegade Conover.

"Glad you won, Vinton," was the remark of several of Hiltz's supporters. "I didn't vote for you, you know, because I'd given my word to Hiltz, but I'm glad you beat."

Then the room emptied and Dan and Arthur followed the others out through the corridor, where the news had already spread. Dan had to stop many times to be shaken by the hand or pounded on the back, but finally he was free to hurry to the gymnasium and get into his togs for afternoon practice. Arthur went with him.

"But what I don't see," said Dan perplexedly, "is how I got fifteen. I had only fourteen that I knew of."

"I can tell you," answered Arthur. "The fifteenth was Simms. He stopped me on the way out a minute ago. 'I concluded you were right, Thompson,' he said. 'I don't like Dan Vinton much, but I guess he's a heap better than Jake Hiltz. So I voted your way.'"

"Simms! Well, I'm much obliged to him, although, as it happened, I didn't need his vote. I wonder what became of Conover? I'd hate to be in his shoes when Hiltz finds him!"

"Oh, Conover's a pill, anyway. He probably forgot all about the election. For my part, I don't care what Jake does to him!"

The mystery of Conover's disappearance was explained later, however, when between the two short practice halves Dan shared Tom's blanket on the side-line.

"They tell me you won, Dan," said Tom. "Glad to hear it; glad you licked Jake Hiltz. Close, was it?"

"I got fifteen to his thirteen."

"Fifteen! I thought you said you were sure of only fourteen."

"I did; and I was. But a fellow named Simms came over to me at the last moment." Tom chuckled.

"That's a joke on me, then. Know a chap with rusty hair and spectacles named Conover?"

"Only by sight. He was one of Hiltz's fellows and didn't show up. I don't know what happened to him. Hiltz is crazy mad, I guess. He sent a fellow out to hunt Conover up, but he wasn't to be found."

"Guess they didn't look in the right place," said Tom with a grin.

"Why? What do you know about it?"

"I know where Conover was from a quarter past two to twenty minutes past three," replied Tom with a twinkle.

"You do? Where?"

"In Number 7 Dudley."

"*What?* In your room? Look here, Tom, what have you been up to?"

"Well, I *thought* I was up to helping you get elected, but it seems that I might just as well have spared myself the trouble."

"Do you mean that you—you——"

Tom nodded.

"Exactly. I knew Conover was a chess fiend, and so this morning, after you told me how you stood, I called on him and invited him to play a game with me after dinner. He was pleased to death. I let him have things his own way, of course, and at three I told him that I hated to spoil the game but that it was time for him to go over and cast his vote. I guess he thought I was trying to rattle him. Anyway, he said he didn't want to vote and wasn't going to. So I thought he knew his own mind, and didn't say any more about it. And then, at twenty after, I started in and did him up. He can't play chess any more than—than Alf can!"

"Tom, you're a wonder!" laughed Dan. "That's the best joke I've heard in a year. It was mighty decent of you, though," he continued seriously, "and I appreciate it."

"Oh, that's all right. I had my fun, too."

"But, just the same, I'm rather glad I got Simms's vote, for I don't think I'd have liked being elected that way."

Tom only grunted.

CHAPTER VIII
AT SOUND VIEW

Mr. Pennimore's return to Sound View was delayed a week, and so it was after Dan's success at the election when Gerald was summoned to the telephone in the school office one morning and found his father at the other end of the line. And it was three nights later that Dan and Tom and Alf took dinner with Gerald and Mr. Pennimore.

The Steamship King was a rather small man of fifty-four, with the face of a scholar rather than of a successful financier and business man. His black eyes were thoughtful and kindly, and his dark hair was as yet only slightly grizzled at the temples. The guests of the evening were very fond of him, and their liking was returned. Gerald's mother had died when he was a few months old, and he was the only child. Until entering Yardley at the beginning of the second term last year he had been all his life in the care of governesses and tutors, with his father keeping an anxious eye on him. The result was only what might have been expected. He had been coddled far too much and a trifle spoiled. But Yardley had done him good. Mr. Pennimore acknowledged that readily and had more than once thanked Dan for having been the cause of Gerald's choice of that school. Even before his son's entrance there Mr. Pennimore had done a good deal for the school, and now that Gerald swore allegiance to the dark blue, he was ready and anxious to do much more, and it was only half a secret that when Gerald graduated there was to be a new and very wonderful dormitory erected to the left of Dudley Hall, and that with the building was to go a generous donation to be used for the general enlargement of the school.

The Pennimore family consisted only of Mr. Pennimore and Gerald, although the big house was filled with servants. To-night the small round table in the center of the big dining room held a very merry quintet. The boys wore their dinner jackets, and wore them with quite an air—all save Tom; Tom looked and doubtless felt very uncomfortable behind his starched shirt-bosom and straining waistcoat. There was little formality at that dinner, for the boys had adopted Mr. Pennimore as one of themselves, a sort of honorary member of Yardley. Mr. Pennimore had to be told all the news, and they each took a hand in bringing history down to date for his benefit. Alf's account of the election amused him vastly, and he looked across at Tom with a twinkle in his black eyes.

"Tom," he said, "you have the making of a politician; I can see that. And I don't know of a better field for politics of the kind you displayed the other day than your own home State of New Jersey — with the possible exception of Delaware and Pennsylvania."

"I've always thought," remarked Alf, allowing the butler to help him to a third slice of chicken, "that Tom would make a dandy alderman. I saw an alderman once and he looked just like Tom — sort of big and lazy."

"You wait till I get you outside," growled Tom.

"Now tell me about football," said their host. "I feel quite honored at having three gridiron heroes at my table at once. Going to whip Broadwood again this year?"

"You bet we are!" declared Gerald emphatically.

"We'd stand a better chance, sir," said Tom, "if we had a good quarter back and a good captain."

"Eh? But I thought that — I thought Alf was — was —" Mr. Pennimore looked about the table bewilderedly, and Gerald broke into laughter.

"That's just Tom's joke, sir. Alf *is* captain and quarter. And he's a dandy, too!"

"Oh, I see." Mr. Pennimore joined the laughter. "I thought I wasn't mistaken about it. And you play end, don't you, Dan? And Tom, here, is——"

"Water carrier," interrupted Alf pleasantly. "Quite correct, sir. And one of the best we've ever had — when he doesn't go to sleep and fall into the pail."

"Tom's right half back, sir," said Gerald, "and you mustn't mind what they say about the team. It's a mighty good team, and it's going to lick spots out of Broadwood in just about two weeks."

"I'm glad to hear it, son. Has the team had a good season so far, Alf?"

"Only fair, sir. We won from Greenburg, Forrest Hill and St. John's, tied Carrel's and lost to Porter and Brewer. The Brewer game ought to have been ours, though. The referee gave them a touchdown they didn't make. The ball was dead about twenty yards from our goal and a Brewer half picked it up and ran over with it."

"But didn't you—ah—protest?"

"Until I was black in the face," replied Alf disgustedly. "But it didn't do any good. The referee was a man they'd picked up somewhere and he was punk. They say he's a baseball umpire. Maybe he is; he certainly isn't a football referee."

"And who do you play Saturday?" asked Mr. Pennimore.

"Nordham, sir. It's our last game before we tackle Broadwood."

"And have they a good team this year?"

"One of the best ever, sir. They've got a fellow named Warren—he was center for Princeton last year—helping coach over there. They say he's a wonder."

"Well," said Dan, "we've got a Yale man coming down to-morrow to help us. And Alf's brother is coming, too, for a couple of days."

"If he can get away," grumbled Alf. "He makes me tired. He made all sorts of promises last year and now he just squeals."

"For my part," remarked Tom, "I think Broadwood's going to give us fits this year. She's got a dandy team, good coaches and we have to play her on her grounds."

"There's a good deal in that," agreed Dan. "I mean in playing away from home."

"Well, we will do the best we can," said Alf cheerfully. "I wonder if I might have some more of the egg plant, sir?"

"There's one thing we have to cheer us up," said Tom, "and that is that our captain is still able to peck at a little food."

"I'm very glad he is," replied Mr. Pennimore with a smile. "And I'd like to see you and Dan doing a little better. Have some more of the chicken, won't you, Tom?"

"No, sir, thanks. I eat very little."

Alf made a choking sound that indicated suppressed laughter.

"Don't take any more chicken," advised Gerald. "There's a salad yet and then some dandy ice cream. And I know you like ice cream, Tom."

"It's one of the few things I can relish," answered Tom with a grin. "I have a very delicate stomach."

"So has an ostrich," jeered Alf.

"Another chap and I fed an ostrich on celluloid campaign buttons once," said Tom reminiscently. "It was at the Zoo. We had our pockets full of Bryan buttons and the ostrich seemed to like them tremendously. I guess he ate about forty of 'em."

"What happened to him?" asked Dan, laughingly.

"I never heard. I guess he became a Bryanite, though."

After dinner there was a comfortable hour in the big library in front of the fire, for the evenings were getting chilly those days, and then the four boys said good night and piled themselves into the automobile and were taken humming back to school.

Yardley had little difficulty with the Nordham Academy team on the following Saturday, sending it down in defeat to the tune of 17 to 0 and thereby earning consolation for what had happened last year when Nordham, with a spry and tricky team, had played her to a tie. Football was in the air now. In fact, Yardley was obsessed with athletics, for not only was the gridiron contest with her hated rival imminent but there was also the question of cross-country supremacy to settle.

On Wednesday morning Andy Ryan sent his charges over the full course for the first time and, although he never gave out the time, he was well pleased. In that run Gerald, who had been doing better at every trial, finished seventh among the twelve who ran. (Garson was out of the team for good with a torn leg muscle sustained in a class football game.) Word filtered into Yardley that Broadwood expected to make a clean sweep next Saturday by winning both in the morning and afternoon. But Yardley laughed scornfully and held three football mass meetings and whooped things up until the enthusiasm was deafening. Cheers and songs were practiced and Dan's contribution made a great success. (Alf's verse, by the way, was not added.) Studies suffered a good deal that last week and the faculty almost called a mass meeting of its own to protest against the students' neglect of lessons. "Kilts," whose real name was Mr. McIntyre and who taught mathematics, shook his head a lot those days and predicted dire things when examination time arrived. But sufficient unto the day was the evil thereof, and just now the one thing in life was to witness the double humiliation of the Green.

The Cross-Country Team had its last work on Thursday when it was sent over half the course at a little more than an amble, and the Eleven held its last practice that afternoon. The Second Team disbanded to the cheers of the students and went capering off the field, glad that their period of hard work and hard knocks was at an end. The First went through signal drill while the spectators cheered them collectively and individually and finally trotted away, leaving the field for the last time that year. The next afternoon the football team and the runners went for a sail on Mr. Pennimore's big steam yacht. It wasn't an ideal day for cruising about the sound, for there was a cold east wind and a lowering sky, but the fellows took along plenty of sweaters and blankets and enjoyed it immensely. The deck of the *Princess* looked like an Indian encampment with all those blue-and-gray blankets dotted about. Mr. Pennimore didn't accompany them, although pressed to do so. "You'll have a better time by yourselves," he declared. "You won't want any old chaps like me on hand."

There was one last, final, ecstatic meeting in the assembly hall on Friday night at which speeches, if you could call them such, were made by Coach Payson and his assistant, by Captain Loring, by Trainer Ryan, by Captain Maury, of the Cross-Country Team, and by Mr. Bendix on behalf of the faculty. Every speaker predicted success, which was just as well, since one might as well talk hopefully even if

Winning His "Y": A Story of School Athletics

they don't feel so, and was cheered to the echo. The Glee Club and the Banjo and Mandolin Club were on hand to supply music and enthusiasm reigned supreme until long after the usual bedtime. And then at ten thirty the next morning the whole student body set out for the start of the cross-country race.

CHAPTER IX
THE CROSS-COUNTRY MEET

The old Cider Mill, a dilapidated two-story building from whose roof and walls the rotting shingles were fast falling away, stood — and for that matter still stands — on the Broadwood road a mile from the river bridge. Meeker's Marsh edges up to the road there and a sluggish creek meanders by it and flows through a runway at the back of the mill before joining the river above Loon Island. The mill is no longer in use and its sagging floors and decaying timbers render prowling through its twilit mysteries an unsafe diversion. Like most deserted and isolated country buildings it has gained the reputation of being haunted. No one, however, takes the report very seriously, and, for that matter, it would be an especially healthy and sturdy ghost who would risk haunting a place which affords so little protection from the weather. At night, with the moonlight throwing strange shadows about it, one might well view it askance, but on a sunshiny November forenoon there is nothing uncanny in its appearance. On the contrary, it is rather picturesque, with the moss tinging the shingles and the weeds and bushes crowding about its door.

It was at the old Cider Mill that the start of the cross-country race was to be made. From there the course led up the Broadwood road for a mile, crossed the fields and hills southward for three quarters of a mile, found the road to Greenburg, passed through that town on a back street, continued to the fork near the river bridge, turned north again past the starting point and finished a mile beyond toward Broadwood. Taken as a whole, the four-mile course was not a difficult one, since only about a fourth of the distance lay off the roads. Each school entered ten men, of whom only the first seven to finish were to count in the result, the first to be credited with one point, the second with two, the third with three, and so on, the team scoring the lowest number of points with its first seven runners to win the race.

Ryan chose his ten runners from the dozen at his disposal on the showing made during the last fortnight, and both Gerald and Jake Hiltz were given places, while Henderson and Groom, neither of whom had been doing at all well of late, were left disconsolate outside the ranks. Gerald had been hoping for a place and more than half expecting it, so he was not surprised when Ryan read his name off with the others, who were Captain Maury, Goodyear, Norcross, Wagner, French, Felder, Thompson and Sherwood. Goodyear and Wagner were believed to be Yardley's best runners, with Captain Maury a close third, and the Dark Blue was hoping strongly that Goodyear would wrest first place away from the Broadwood crack, Scott, although the latter had a reputation as a distance runner which no one dared dispute.

At a few minutes before eleven the teams lined up in two ranks across the road and the rules governing the race were explained to them. Gerald found himself in the second rank between Felder, of his own team, and a tall, fast-looking Broadwood youth. The Broadwood runners were very neat and jaunty in their new costumes of dark-green shirts and white trunks. Yardley, who had not considered the matter of attire until too late, wore white shirts and trunks with a blue ribbon across the breast. On the backs of the contestants were pinned their numbers. Most of the spectators at the starting point owned allegiance to Yardley, although a sprinkling of Broadwood fellows had journeyed over to see the teams get away. It was at the finish, however, that Broadwood had congregated most of her supporters. At two minutes after the hour the word was given and the twenty runners trotted away from the line.

A four-mile cross-country race isn't exactly a sprint and there was no rush for the front, no jockeying for position, such as takes place at the beginning of a half or quarter. There was plenty of time for spurting after the fellows had got their pace and their wind. Gerald found himself in the middle of the group after the first few hundred feet had been run, with Jake Hiltz just ahead of him. I'm forced to confess that Gerald's ambition that morning was not so much to assist in a victory over Broadwood as it was to defeat Jake Hiltz, and even at the start of the contest Gerald suited his pace to Hiltz's and settled down to run that youth off his feet irrespective of what happened to anyone else. It was easy enough going for the first mile, for the Broadwood road is well traveled and fairly level. As they approached the point where the course left the highway and entered the fields, and where they were to finish later on, they were met with cheers from the crowd of Broadwood spectators lining the road there.

"Go it, Scott!" was the cry. "Beat 'em out! You can do it!"

The runners turned into the field with the Broadwood cheer ringing in their ears. By this time the group had lengthened to a procession, with Scott, the Broadwood crack, leading Goodyear, of Yardley, by a dozen feet. Then came Captain Maury and Arthur Thompson, and two Broadwood fellows close on their heels. Farther back Gerald was keeping a yard or so behind Jake Hiltz. He had found his second wind now and, although he was the youngest entry in the race, his form aroused several comments from the audience at the turn.

"Look at the kid," said one fellow. "Gee, Yardley must be hard up for runners to put him in. Say, he can run, though, can't he? Isn't that a pretty stride of his? Wonder who he is."

"That's young Pennimore," some one informed him. "John T.'s son. They say he will have more money than he will know what to do with when he grows up. The old man's a multi-millionaire, whatever that is!"

"Well, he certainly has a pretty way of using his legs," said a third, "kid or no kid."

It wasn't so easy now that they had the rough, frosty turf under foot, and soon they were taking a long hill. The stragglers began to drop farther behind. Between Scott and Goodyear and the next group the distance lengthened. Thompson had dropped back and two Broadwood runners and Wagner, of Yardley, had passed him. Hiltz and Gerald were well toward the last. Once Hiltz glanced back and saw Gerald behind him. "Hello, Miss Nancy," he called over his shoulder. "Aren't your little legs tired?" Gerald didn't waste his breath answering. At the top of the hill Gerald looked back. The last half dozen fellows were strung out for an eighth of a mile, some of them, noticeably Norcross of Yardley, making hard work of the slope. A couple of stone walls had to be negotiated next and Arthur Thompson, who had fallen back to within a dozen yards of Gerald, tried to take the second one at a jump. His foot struck in going over, however, and he fell on the other side and measured his length in a patch of brambles. Gerald paused as he reached him. Arthur was climbing slowly and rather dazedly to his feet.

"Aren't hurt, are you?" asked Gerald anxiously.

"No, but I've got a beast of a stitch in my side, Gerald. I'm afraid I'm out of it." Arthur trotted along with his hand on his ribs. "That hill did it. I was all right until then."

"Take it easy. Maybe you'll get over it," said Gerald. "Let's move up; I don't want Hiltz to get too much of a lead."

"You go on," answered Arthur with a groan. "I'll go slow for awhile and see if the pain lets up. Maybe I'll manage to get a place."

"All right," answered Gerald. "Don't give up."

Hiltz had gained most of a hundred yards, but Gerald set to work doggedly and unhurriedly, and by the time they had skirted the woods and had found the Greenburg road he was once more on Hiltz's heels, much to that youth's surprise and displeasure. The race was half run now and Scott and Goodyear were still going easily and well within two yards of each other. But they had pulled ahead of the rest and were far down the road when Gerald felt the hard ground under foot again. The outlying houses of the town came into sight and soon they were speeding along a back street between rows of tenements and laborers' cottages. Hiltz and Gerald were running twelfth and thirteenth now and the pace had begun to tell on both. Hiltz had eased up perceptibly and Gerald could hear his deep gasps for breath. Gerald was in better shape, but nevertheless he was not at all ill pleased when Hiltz began to slow down. Before they had left the town two Broadwood fellows and French of Yardley passed them. French was making hard work of it, although he tried to grin bravely as he called: "Come on, you fellows! We've got it cinched!" A quarter of a mile farther on, however, they overtook him walking at the side of the road with drooping head.

"Sorry," called Gerald as he trotted by.

French lifted a drawn, tired face, nodded and smiled wryly.

Then the bridge was in sight and, this side of it, the abrupt turn into the Broadwood road that announced the beginning of the final mile.

Gerald was watching Hiltz sharply now, wondering whether to try him with a spurt. As they reached the turn he made up his mind and, quickening his pace, ran inside of his rival and gained the lead. But Hiltz, although taken by surprise, wasn't dead yet, and in the next fifty yards he had passed Gerald and regained the lead. And Gerald, quite satisfied, settled down into his former pace and plugged away with aching muscles and tortured lungs. Far up the road Scott and Goodyear were struggling for supremacy, two white specks in the distance.

CHAPTER X
AT THE FINISH

As soon as the runners had gotten away the spectators at the old Cider Mill set out along the country road for the finish, a mile away toward Broadwood. Some few had bicycles, but the most of them walked. Among the latter were Dan and Alf and Tom. Paul Rand had started out with them, but somewhere along the way he had fallen in with friends and had deserted them. When they reached the finish they found a comfortable, sunny place on the hillside and spread their sweaters.

"It's warming up," said Alf, "and I guess we won't catch cold. I don't want any of you fellows stiff this afternoon, though. We'd better not sit here too long, I fancy."

"Oh, this is all right," muttered Tom, squatting down. "What time do the coaches start for Broadwood, Alf?"

"One thirty. And luncheon's at twelve forty-five prompt. What time is it now?"

"Eleven twenty-five," answered Dan. "Say, who's going to umpire? Didn't Payson say that Wallace couldn't come?"

"Yes. I don't know who they'll get. It's up to Broadwood. They've got two or three men over there that'll be all right."

They talked over the afternoon's game for awhile, contrary to Payson's instructions, and then Mills, the Broadwood captain, spied them and joined the group. Mills was a big, broad-shouldered chap of twenty, a splendid guard and a splendid fellow as well, and every man who had ever played against him liked him thoroughly. He and Alf shook hands, and then Tom greeted him and Alf introduced Dan.

"Glad to meet you, Mr. Vinton," said Mills warmly. "I don't believe, though, that we need an introduction. I guess we remember each other from last year, don't we? Anyhow, I remember you—to my sorrow."

Dan smiled.

"I hope you'll remember us all to your sorrow this afternoon," he said.

"I don't," laughed Mills. "Well, what do you say about it, Loring?" he asked, turning to the rival captain. "How's it coming out?"

"If I knew I'd tell you," replied Alf dryly. "Honestly, Mills, I wouldn't attempt to guess. You fellows have got a ripping good team; we all know that; and we've got a pretty fair one too. And there you are. You've had some good coaching this year, haven't you?"

Mills nodded.

"No kick there," he said. "And we've got some good players. Well, I want to win, and I guess you do, too, Loring. However it comes out it's going to be a good game. I wouldn't miss it for a million dollars. By the way, you fellows are going to use the gym this year. We've fixed it so you can have the upstairs floor. That all right?"

"It's fine, thanks," answered Alf gratefully. "It beats trying to keep warm in one of those confounded coaches. It's mighty decent of you chaps."

"Not a bit. I don't see why we haven't always done that. I guess the time's going by when it's the style to make the other fellow as uncomfortable as possible in the hope that it'll affect his playing. Say, you had a rough deal at Brewer, didn't you? What was the matter with that referee? I sent Foley and Robinson over to see the game and they were telling me about it."

"Oh, he was just crazy under foot like a radish," answered Alf disgustedly. "The ball was dead and he didn't know it."

"Too bad. By the way, how's this stunt coming out?" asked Mills with a nod toward the finish line.

"Oh, we have this affair cinched," said Tom lazily. "We've filled all our runners with oxygen and put motors on 'em. You can't beat 'em, Mills."

"I guess not, in that case. Well, I must mosey along. See you all this afternoon, fellows, and I hope we'll have a good, clean game. And if you win, why, it's all right—until next time. Only I won't be here next time."

"Same with me," said Alf. "But maybe we'll have a crack at each other in college, Mills. You're for Princeton, I suppose?"

"Yes, if I pass! You going up to Yale?" Alf nodded.

"Same 'if.'"

"Well, good-by," said Mills, nodding. "Some of those runners ought to be turning up pretty soon, I suppose."

"He's a mighty decent chap," mused Alf, when the visitor had strolled away toward where the Broadwood contingent was grouped at the finish. "Wonder why we didn't get him at Yardley."

"You can't have all the good things," murmured Tom. "You've got me, you know."

"Yes, I do know it, you old chump." There was a cry from a youth who was watching the road from the vantage point of a tree limb and the trio scrambled to their feet, rescued their sweaters and pushed their way through the crowd which was struggling for positions along the road.

"There they come!" was the cry. "Two of them!"

"That's Scott!" shrieked a Broadwood youngster.

"And the other one's Goodyear, or I'll eat my hat!" muttered Alf. "Say, who's got a piece of paper. Let's keep score on them as they finish. We can't wait around here until those silly judges get through figuring it up or we'll never make school in time for luncheon."

"Here's an envelope you can have," said Dan. "Got your pen?"

"Yes. Look at Goodyear, Tom! He's passing him, by Jove! Come on, you Goody! Eat him up!"

Nearer and nearer came the leaders, heads back now and arms hanging listlessly. It was a gallant fight for four miles in time that set a dual record for the distance that has never yet been surpassed over the course. A hundred feet from the finish the two were running side by side. At half the distance Goodyear went ahead. Scott tried his best to pull down the scant lead, but the Yardley man held it to the line, crossing a bare two feet to the good and securing for the Dark Blue the individual honors of the meet, no matter what might happen later. Yardley's cheers filled the air, and, after the first moment of disappointment, Broadwood added a hearty cheer for her rival to the applause she accorded Scott.

"Yardley, 1; Broadwood, 2," murmured Alf, setting the figures down. "So far so good. Any more in sight, Tom?"

"Don't see any, but there's a lot of chumps on the road. Some one ought to make 'em keep off."

There was a wait then until the next group appeared. At sight of them Yardley again broke into shouts, for the runner ahead wore the blue stripe.

"It's Maury," said Alf. "I know the way he runs. The others are both Broadwood chaps."

Maury finished well ahead and Andrews and Crossett, of Broadwood, got fourth and fifth place respectively.

"What does that make it?" asked Dan, leaning over Alf's shoulder as the latter set the figures down.

"Make it four to their eleven, but they've finished three men to our two. Who's this coming?"

"Two Yardleys with no one else near," cried Dan. "I don't know who they are. Yes, I do, though. The first man's Wagner."

"And the next is Sherwood," added Tom. "And there come two of our hated rivals, and I hope they choke."

Wagner and Sherwood trotted across the line and subsided into the arms of their friends, limp and tuckered. Then came Holder and White, both wearers of the Green, and after that there were no more for several minutes.

"The score, gentlemen," announced Alf, frowning over his scrawls, "is Yardley, 17; Broadwood, 28."

"Great!" cried Dan, with a caper.

"Maybe, but they've got five men in to our four."

"That can't be right," Tom objected.

"Can't it, Mr. Fixit? Why not? Look here. Yardley gets first, third, sixth and seventh places, and that makes seventeen. See? And Broadwood gets second, fourth, fifth, eighth and ninth, which foots up twenty-eight. I guess we've got to get the next runner in, fellows."

"Not necessarily," began Tom. But just then a shout went up and the crowd moved forward again. Far up the road trotted a single runner and Yardley sighed her relief, for his shirt shone white in the sunlight. A moment later a second runner appeared, a dark-shirted youth who, in spite of the distance between him and the man in front, seemed determined to overtake him.

"But he can't do it," whispered Dan half aloud. "Our chap's got too much lead. Why, that's Thompson, Alf."

"So it is. Good for him! Come on, you Thompson. Never mind about looking back. Hit it up!"

But Arthur was still too far away to hear this advice. The Broadwood runner was gaining in a way that would have elicited warm admiration from the trio at any other time. Arthur was plainly on his last legs. Twenty yards from the line he stumbled, recovered himself and came on, only to fall in a heap finally in the middle of the road some ten yards from the finish.

CHAPTER XI
BY ONE POINT

"Don't touch him!" was the cry as sympathetic friends rushed to Arthur's assistance. "Let him alone! Let him finish! Come on, Thompson! You can do it! Here he comes!"

Broadwood was yelling madly, encouragingly to her plucky runner, who, seeing his adversary's plight, was making one final effort to wrest the victory from him. But he was still yards behind when Arthur found his feet unsteadily, cast a look to the rear, and limped, swaying and clutching, toward the finish. Once across it he sprawled face down in the road before willing arms could reach him, and the Broadwood runner, crossing the line the next instant, stumbled over him and measured his length, too, on the ground.

"Bully work!" commented Alf, his pen busy again. "That gives us tenth place and Broadwood eleventh. Say, this is getting rather too close to be interesting. What we need is two more runners just about now, before Broadwood finishes her last man."

"And one of them is coming," said Dan excitedly. "It's a Yardley runner, isn't it, Tom? See his white shirt?"

"Yes, it's a Yardleyite, all right," Tom muttered.

"Sure?" asked Alf, trying to glimpse the distant road. "Then that makes our sixth man and the score is—by Jove, fellows! What do you think?"

"We don't think; what is it? Are we ahead?"

"We're just even; 39 to 39!"

"Oh, your score is crazy," said Tom.

But Alf went over it, while Felder finished amid the plaudits of his schoolmates, and found it correct.

"That means, then," commented Tom, "that we've got to get the next runner in or lose the shindig. I guess I'll take a nap until the excitement's over. I have a weak heart."

"That's right," agreed Dan nervously, "this *is* sort of suspensous."

"Whatever that may be," added Alf. "Gee, I wish some one would come along and get it over. What time is it? How long will it take us to get back? What are they cheering about now?"

"Just to keep their courage up, I guess," answered Tom.

The minutes dragged along while anxious eyes searched the distant bend of the road impatiently. And then, finally, a shout went up from the throng.

"Broadwood! Broadwood!" shrieked the Green's supporters.

"That right?" asked Alf. Dan nodded.

"Then we're dished!"

"Hold on, Alf, there's another fellow just behind him. Never say die!"

Yardley's cheers drowned Broadwood's now, for the second runner was all in white and the distance between him and the man ahead was not so great, after all. The crowd flowed over onto the road, amid the appeals of the officials for "Track, please! Track! Everyone off the road! Let them finish! Give them room!"

Far up the road sped Green and Dark Blue, but as they came nearer and nearer it was evident that Dark Blue was gradually lessening the distance between him and his foe. Inch by inch, foot by foot the Yardley runner conquered the space, and a hundred yards from the finish he was almost within reach of the Broadwood man. Dan gave a whoop of delight.

"Do you see who it is, Tom?" he cried.

"No, but he's a little cuss. Say, it isn't——"

"Yes, it is, it's Gerald!"

"Get out!" gasped Alf.

"It is, though, isn't it, Tom?"

"Gerald for a dollar!" cried Tom delightedly. "And he will get him yet!"

"The plucky little beggar!" exclaimed Alf. "Can he do it? Think of the race depending on him, Dan! Wouldn't that jar you? Is he gaining?"

"I—I don't believe so," muttered Dan anxiously. "He cut down a lot, but he's just about holding his place now. He runs well, too, and looks fresher than the other chap. Oh, gee, Alf, why doesn't he try harder?"

A groan went up from the Yardley watchers, for the Broadwood runner had suddenly sprung away and now a good four or five yards separated him from Gerald, and the finish was almost at hand.

After that first attempt to leave Hiltz behind Gerald had subsided into a pace that kept him just at the other's heels. There was time enough yet, for it was evident that Hiltz was fast getting weary. And then, a minute or two later, Arthur Thompson drew up to them, passed them and went ahead, running at a good speed but looking pretty white of face save where a flaming disk of crimson burned on each cheek. Gerald saw his opportunity and seized it. He sprang forward, passed Hiltz and fell in behind Arthur, letting the latter make pace for him. Hiltz made one despairing effort to follow and then gave up the struggle, trotting along for a minute more and finally subsiding to a walk as the two others left him behind.

The last mile was almost half covered when Bailey, of Broadwood, overtook them, running as though he had not already put three and a half miles behind him. Thompson accepted the challenge and the two gradually drew away from Gerald who tried to keep up with them but found it impossible. Then Felder passed slowly, turning to give Gerald a drawn but encouraging smile. And then the last turn was in sight. Gerald glanced back to see if Hiltz was dangerously near. He wasn't, but the tall Broadwood chap who had stood beside him at the start was coming up hard. Gerald had scant idea now of figuring in the result of the contest, but since Hiltz was out of the running the newcomer offered him other rivalry. So Gerald let out another notch, more to see what he could do than for any other reason, and for awhile kept the Broadwood man behind. But Gerald didn't care a great deal, now that he had worsted Hiltz, and so presently, when Loughan, of Broadwood, spurted, he only half-heartedly contested honors with him, being content to fall in behind and to ease up sufficiently to get some relief from the ache and pull at his tired lungs.

He expected to find, when the turn was past, that the race would be over and thought to meet his fellows homeward bound on the road. But a quite different sight met his wearied gaze. Off there at the finish the road was black with fellows and the sound of their cheering came plainly to him. His heart leaped. Perhaps, after all, he was still in the running! At least, he wouldn't chance it. Up came his head then and his legs began to twinkle faster over the rutted road. Little by little he reduced Loughan's lead, delighted to find that he still had strength and breath in his tired, aching body. Quite clearly now the wild, imploring cheers of Yardley and Broadwood reached him and he no longer doubted that something, whether much or little he didn't know, depended on his beating that boy ahead.

The finish was barely a hundred yards distant now and Gerald was almost up to Loughan, and the knowledge came to him that he was in better shape than the other and could win if the distance was only great enough. And then, suddenly, the other bounded forward and in half a dozen strides had opened up as many yards between them. Gerald with a gasp called every muscle and ounce of remaining strength into play and spurted gallantly after him. But the line was coming toward them fast and the distance between blue ribbon and green shirt lessened but slowly. And yet lessen it did, for the Broadwood man had shot his last bolt, and shot it too early, and ten yards from the line Gerald was even with him.

The air was full of sound, deafening, thunderous. Gerald set his eyes on the line and strove to draw away from that bobbing blur of green beside him. Three strides—another—and the green was still there, although how he knew it he couldn't have told, since his eyes never left the finish in all that final agonizing effort. Another stride—and another—and there was a new note in the bedlam of sound. The blur of green was no longer there and the finish line was under foot! If only he could keep his legs a moment, an instant longer. But it was no use! He felt his limbs giving way beneath him; he struggled for breath and fell forward, groping blindly.

Winning His "Y": A Story of School Athletics

But eager arms caught him beyond the line, and at a little distance, Alf, trying hard to keep his pen steady, was setting down the final score:

YARDLEY, 52; BROADWOOD, 53.

Gerald had won the Cross-Country by one point.

SUMMARY

	Yardley	Broadwood
1 Goodyear	1	
2 Scott		2
3 Maury	3	
4 Crossett		4
5 Andrews	5	
6 Wagner	6	
7 Sherwood		7
8 Holder		8
9 White	9	
10 Thompson	10	
11 Bailey		11

12	Felder	12
13	Pennimore	13
14	Loughan	14
	— —	— —
	Total 52	53

CHAPTER XII
OFF TO BROADWOOD

It was a very tired and rather sick Gerald that bumped home in the coach with his head on Arthur Thompson's shoulder. He was thoroughly used up, and that was all there was to it, he told himself. If he hadn't had to make that spurt in the last quarter of a mile he would, he was certain, have finished the race quite fresh. But the final demand on his powers had been almost too much for him. Not that he regretted it for an instant. He was mighty glad he had beat Loughan and so secured the contest for Yardley. In fact, he was secretly a little bit proud of himself, which emotion was, after all, quite excusable. It was his first real athletic triumph, and it had been won in the face of the whole school. He guessed that now they wouldn't believe Hiltz's lie about his having cheated in the trial run! He glanced down the length of the swaying coach to where Hiltz, looking rather the worse for his morning's exertions, was sitting in the far corner. He didn't seem happy, Gerald thought, and for the first time since he had left Hiltz behind in the race the recollection of his victory over his rival brought no thrill. After all, to have defeated Hiltz was a small thing compared with having won the day for Yardley!

If Gerald was a little proud of himself, the school was even prouder. Every fellow who won a place in the event came in for his meed of praise and admiration from his fellows, but Gerald's case was unique. As Joe Chambers said, he was "such a little tyke, you see!" And while all the others, Goodyear and Maury and Wagner and Sherwood and Thompson and Felder, had each helped to win the meet, it was Gerald, the youngest chap participating, who had at the last possible moment snatched it out of the fire. He was the real hero of the day, and so they had clustered about him and tried to shake his hand or thump him on the back and had cheered him over and over and for a minute or two had acted quite like crazy folks. Gerald had been only dimly aware of this, however, and the cheering had seemed to come from a long way off. It was only when the last man had finished and Arthur had half lifted him into the coach that he had regained his wandering faculties.

Winning His "Y": A Story of School Athletics

About him the fellows were talking merrily, discussing and explaining and questioning. Goodyear told how Scott had tried to make him take the lead at the third mile and how he had refused the honor, preferring to let the Broadwood crack choose the pace, and how Scott had grumbled at intervals all the rest of the way, accusing him of being a "quitter."

"I was awfully surprised to see you go by," said Gerald rather weakly to Arthur.

"I was surprised myself," laughed Arthur. "Gee, I never had such a stitch in my side as I had to-day. I thought for awhile that I was surely down and out. But after I'd taken it easy for a bit it got a whole lot better and finally it went away altogether and I felt finer than I had since the start. If the race had been a mile or so longer I guess I could have finished way up front. Well, you certainly smeared Jake all right, didn't you? When I came across you two it looked as though you'd sworn undying friendship and wouldn't be parted for anything. You were putting your spikes down in his footsteps every time."

"I had him beaten from the beginning," said Gerald, "but he didn't know it. I let him make the pace and all I had to do was to stay with him and let him worry."

"And I guess he worried, judging from the way he's looking now. Guess he hasn't stopped yet. He's probably wondering how he's going to explain it, after his story about the trial. I think I'll ask him, Gerald; bet you he will tell us he had a stitch in his side."

"Please, I'd rather you didn't," begged Gerald. But Arthur either didn't hear or didn't heed.

"Say, Jake," he called, "what happened to you to-day?"

Hiltz looked up scowlingly. "Had a pain," he answered morosely. "I'd have finished ahead of you if I hadn't."

"Too bad," said Arthur sympathetically while a quiet smile traveled up and down the coach. "I had one myself and know what it's like. Anyone see Norcross? He was out of it almost from the start. Guess he wasn't feeling very fit to-day."

"He went home long ago," said Felder. "I met him just as we made the turn down there. Told me he was all in, and looked it, too."

"Too bad," said Maury. "He's a good runner when he's in shape. Well, fellows, we must do this again next year, now that we've got started. Ryan says we ought to keep up the interest by holding a school run in the spring and getting all the fellows to come out for it."

"Might have a class race," suggested Goodyear.

"Bully idea," Sherwood agreed. "I don't see why we shouldn't build up a good cross-country reputation here at Yardley."

"I don't care so much about the reputation," put in Wagner, "if we can only beat Broadwood two years out of three."

"Why not three out of three?" asked Maury with a laugh.

"Oh, we mustn't discourage them. They might quit, you know."

"No, they wouldn't," said Sherwood. "Broadwood's no quitter. I'll say that for her."

"I thank you on behalf of our defeated rival," said Maury, with a polite bow. "You're going over to the game, aren't you?"

"Rather! I guess every fellow in school is going. There's going to be five coaches, all they could scrape up, and a bunch of us will have to walk."

"I shall borrow Hal's motor cycle," remarked Felder carelessly. Goodyear punched him playfully in the ribs.

"Over my dead body, sonny! I need that myself."

"Then you may take me on the handle bars."

"All right, if you'll stand the risk, I will. Got your life insured?"

"Yes, I put thirty cents on it only yesterday. The policy is payable to you, Hal."

"My, I don't see how you got so much!" said Maury. "Wonderful what risks these insurance companies will take nowadays to get business, isn't it?"

Winning His "Y": A Story of School Athletics

"All out, gentlemen!" called Goodyear. "Yardley, Yardley! One hour for dinner!"

Everyone was very happy, for the morning's success was accepted as an augury of an afternoon's victory, and dinner was a noisy and merry affair, so noisy that Mr. Collins, the assistant principal, arose twice in his place at table and informed the room at large that "really, gentlemen, this noise must stop! You are carrying it too far!"

The football team and substitutes had their luncheon early and at half past one their two conveyances were awaiting them. They went off to cheers from as many of their fellows as were not engaged in commons, while those that were scrambled to the windows and shouted from there; and got another rebuke from Mr. Collins. The school at large set off on foot, on bicycle and by coach as soon as dinner was over; all save Gerald and Arthur and young Harry Merrow. They traveled to Broadwood in Mr. Pennimore's big car, Harry Merrow sitting very proudly beside the chauffeur and waving his blue flag all the way.

It was an ideal football day for players and spectators alike. There was an almost cloudless sky above, while around them stretched a green-and-russet world bathed in sunshine. The breeze from the west held a frosty nip, but a good thick sweater was all the extra clothing required to insure comfort. Broadwood was in holiday attire as the machine rolled in at the gate and ascended the curving road past the dormitories. From almost every window a green flag with its white B fluttered, while the front of the gymnasium, which was on the way to the field, was draped in a great green banner with the word Broadwood spelled along its length in startling white letters two feet high.

The automobile had eaten up the miles in quick time and Mr. Pennimore's party was on the scene before the bulk of the audience had arrived. They found a place for the car at one corner of the field, but Gerald and the others voted to see the contest from the side line nearer the middle of the gridiron. The small grand stand began to fill with ladies and their escorts and numerous other automobiles came gingerly across the frosty turf and found positions near Mr. Pennimore's car. By two o'clock the spectators lined the field two deep, while on the roof of the laboratory near at hand and in the windows of that building many Broadwood fellows had found posts of vantage.

Broadwood was first on the field and was cheered enthusiastically by its supporters and politely by the Yardley section which had taken possession of one side of the gridiron. Ten minutes later Yardley trotted on, Alf leading, and then the blue flags had their inning and Yardley cheers arose in volume to the afternoon sky. Broadwood fulfilled the requirements of the occasion with "a regular cheer for Yardley fellows, and make it strong!" And then Yardley yelled "A-a-ay!" in approval and gratification from across the field. And promptly at two thirty Mills led his team to the northern end of the gridiron and Yardley kicked off.

CHAPTER XIII
"FIGHTING FOR OLD YARDLEY"

Yardley	Broadwood
Vinton, l. e.	r. e., Bishop
Coke, l. t.	r. t., Booth
Hadlock, l. g.	r. g., Haines
Fogg, c.	c., Johnson
Merriwell, r. g.	l. g., Mills
Little, r. t.	l. t., Weldon
Dickenson, r. e.	l. e., Corry
Loring, q. b.	q. b., Dowling
Roeder, l. h. b.	r. h. b., Reid
Dyer, r. h. b.	l. h. b., Ayres
Eisner, f. b.	f. b., Rhodes

Coke, the Yardley left tackle, sent the ball spinning from the tee on a long, low kick to Broadwood's two-yard line, where Reid, the Green's right half, ran it back past three white lines before he was stopped. The Broadwood full back went through Merriwell for a clean five yards, to the joy of the Broadwood supporters, but on the next play Roeder threw Reid for a loss and Weldon was forced to kick. Dan received the ball on Broadwood's forty-three yards. Roeder failed to gain through center and Alf punted to Reid, who fumbled, Dan recovering the ball on the twenty-eight-yard line.

Yardley shouted blissfully, for with the pigskin within the shadow of Broadwood's goal and in possession of the Blue a touchdown looked imminent. And after the next play it looked a good deal more so, for Roeder was driven through right tackle eighteen yards, eluding the secondary defense and being pulled and hauled along in a way that brought the Yardley supporters in the stand to their feet. Yardley cheerers demanded a touchdown with wild, exultant voices as the two teams faced each other on the nine-yard line. But Broadwood steadied down and Roeder and Tom between them only made four yards. On the next play Loring tried a forward pass to Little, but the latter failed to reach it and the ball bounded over for a touchback. Broadwood murmured its relief.

Weldon, Broadwood's left tackle, punted out from the twenty-yard line to Eisner, Yardley's full back, who made a dozen yards before he was tackled. Tom made five through right tackle, Dan failed to gain and Roeder missed first down by two yards. The ball went to Broadwood on her forty yards. Broadwood was twice thrown for a loss and punted again, Dan receiving the ball on his forty-four-yard line. He was downed in his tracks by Bishop. Tom and Roeder made eight yards and Alf punted to Reid, who again fumbled to Dickenson, on the Green's thirty-three yards. On the next play Roeder was thrown for a two-yard loss and Yardley was set still farther back for off side. With the ball on the Green's forty yards Alf tried an on-side kick which went to Reid for a fair catch on his twenty-five yards. Ayres made five yards around Dan's end and Rhodes went through center for four more. With one to gain Weldon punted to Dan who caught the ball on his forty-yard line. On the subsequent play Fogg was caught holding and Yardley was set back fifteen yards. Tom made up the distance on a skin-tackle play and then plugged center for nine more, and Yardley cheers arose deafeningly. It was first down almost in the center of the field. Alf worked a pretty forward pass to Coke, which was just long enough to give Yardley first down again, and then Roeder made three yards at left tackle and Dan recovered Alf's fumble on Broadwood's forty-five-yard line. Alf punted outside to Dowling, and after the ball had been brought in at the twenty-five-yard line the Green hammered the Yardley line without much gain, and Weldon returned the ball to Dan in the middle of the gridiron. Eisner punted over the head of the Broadwood quarter and the ball rolled over the line for the second touchback of the game.

From the twenty-yard line Weldon again punted and Dan misjudged the kick and fumbled. Alf, however, was on hand and got the ball before the Broadwood end reached him, tearing off five yards before he was brought down. After that for a while the ball went back and forth between the twenty-five-yard lines until, near the end of the period, Broadwood made two on-side kicks successfully and for the first time in the game had the ball in her possession inside Yardley territory. It was well inside, too, for after the recovery of that second on-side kick by Johnson, the Broadwood center, the pigskin rested on Yardley's eighteen yards. For almost the first time Broadwood had good and sufficient reason for rejoicing, and rejoice she did. The green flags waved wildly and along the side of the field the local enthusiasts capered and shouted. Rhodes made a scant three yards at Little and on a second attempt was thrown for a loss. Captain Mills and his quarter back held a consultation and then Weldon was called back and everyone knew that Broadwood was about to try a goal from field. Weldon placed himself on the twenty-seven-yard line and held his hands out, the ball went back to him on a good pass and he tried a drop kick. But the ball fell short and Dan pulled it down and was not caught until he had wormed and fought his way back to the twenty-eight yards. Yardley yelled its triumph and derision and a depressed stillness encompassed the Broadwood ranks.

Five minutes later, after Alf had punted to Broadwood's thirty-nine yards and Dowling's on-side kick had been recovered by Dan, Yardley set to work and ripped things wide open. There was a blocked punt luckily recovered by Alf, and Payson sent Sommers in in place of Eisner. Sommers was an erratic player, with plenty of strength and football knowledge when it pleased him to show them. He showed both to-day, in the remaining five minutes of the half, for on his first two plunges directly through the center of the Broadwood line he netted fifteen yards and made it first down. Mills was hurt in the second of the rushes and the play was held up for the full two minutes while he recovered. When he got to his feet again Yardley cheered him loudly. From the thirty-seven-yard line Tom went forward for five yards, Roeder took four more and Tom secured first down on Broadwood's twenty-three yards. Yardley was imploring a field goal, but after a moment's hesitation Alf decided that a touchdown was what was needed and to that end attempted a forward pass. But again Little failed and Broadwood got the pigskin eight yards from her goal line. And at that moment time was called for the first half.

"There's nothing to it but Yardley!" cried Gerald as he and Arthur made their way back to the automobile to rejoin Mr. Pennimore. "We put it all over them!"

"Yes, but we had two chances to score and missed them both," objected Arthur.

"Well, Broadwood had one chance and didn't do any better," replied Gerald. "Besides, the play was in her territory all the time except when they worked those two on-side kicks; and that was more luck than anything else!"

"I don't know. The play was pretty even."

"Why, Broadwood didn't make a single first down on rushing!" Gerald scoffed. "And we made at least four."

"Just the same Broadwood will come back hard in the next half. I wish we had managed to score."

"So do I, but I'll bet you we'll just make rings around them in the next half. Isn't Alf playing a dandy game?"

"Great! I never saw him run the team as smoothly, and he's keeping old Broadwood guessing all the time with the plays he's using. Broadwood is sticking to old-fashioned football pretty well; more than she did last year; and if she loses it will be only because the two lines are too nearly even for her to win on line bucking. And Dan's doing great work too. He missed only one punt, and that was a tough one to handle. His backfield work is fine. And I don't think the Broadwood backs got around his end more than once, either."

"It doesn't seem to me that Mills is showing up much," said Gerald.

"Well, it's hard to tell. Sommers got by him twice that I know of and Tom didn't have much trouble with the center of their line. But it's hard to judge of a linesman's work unless you're right on the field there."

"I suppose it is. Hello, dad! Isn't it great?"

"Fine," responded Mr. Pennimore, puffing complacently on his cigar. "Looks as though we'd win, doesn't it, son?"

"Yes, sir. We're going to tie strings to them the next half. Wasn't Dan fine?"

"He was, indeed. And I thought Tom seemed to get along pretty well when he had the ball."

"You bet! Tom always does. He just puts his head down and gives a grunt and *goes through*!"

"That's a good way to do," laughed his father. "Enjoying it, Arthur?"

"Very much, sir. Can you see all right from here?"

"Oh, yes. I stood up on the seat. Nearly fell off once when What's-his-name—Roeder—made that run over there just after the game started. It was beautiful to see the way they pulled him along. It seemed to catch Broadwood napping, didn't it?"

"You bet it did! Isn't it a dandy day for a game?" Gerald climbed into the car and settled down on the back seat and Arthur followed him. Over at the side of the field the Yardley cheer leaders were calling "Yardley this way! Yardley this way!" and the blue flags were massing together back of the ropes. Soon the singing began.

"This is Dan's song," said Gerald eagerly. "Listen, father!

> "'All together! Cheer on cheer!
> Now we're charging down the field!
> See how Broadwood pales with fear,
> Knowing we will never yield!
> Wave on high your banner blue,
> Cheer for comrades staunch and true;
> We are here to die or do,

Fighting for old Yardley!'

"Isn't that great?" demanded Gerald. "Dan wrote the words and his sister made the music."

"The—ah—the music sounds a little bit familiar, doesn't it, though?" inquired Mr. Pennimore with a smile.

"All music does," replied Gerald seriously. "Here's the second verse:

"'All together! Cheer on cheer!
  Victory is ours to-day!
Raise your voices loud and clear!
  Yardley pluck has won the fray!
See, the vanquished foeman quails;
All his vaunted courage fails!
Flaunt the Blue that never pales,
  Fighting for old Yardley!'"

Across the empty field the Broadwood supporters had let their own song die down to listen, and at the end of Yardley's effort they cheered approvingly and generously. But they didn't intend that the enemy should have its own way in matters musical and so came back with their own favorite, "Broadwood Green." They followed that up with the song that Yardley detested most, "What'll We Do?"

"'Not far away there is a school
  That thinks it can play ball, sir.
We'll show it just a trick or two,
We'll show it what our men can do,
And———
  It won't think so this fall, sir!
Oh, what'll we do to Yardley, to Yardley, to Yardley?
Oh, what'll we do to Yardley?
  Well, really, I'd rather not say!'"

Yardley tried to drown the hated words with much cheering and then retaliated with:

"Old Yardley has the men, my boy,
  Old Yardley has the steam,
Old Yardley has the pluck and sand,
  Old Yardley has the team!

Winning His "Y": A Story of School Athletics

Old Yardley can't be beat, my boy,
  She's bound to win the game!
So give a cheer for Yardley and
  Hats off to Yardley's fame!"

A moment later the teams returned and the rival camps strove to surpass each other in their welcomes. It was Broadwood's kick off, and in a moment the ball was high in air, cork screwing against the blue of the afternoon sky. Mills had made the kick and it was a good one, high and far, but his ends were slow in getting down under it and Dan, catching the ball, reeled off sixteen yards before he fell into the clutches of the enemy on his eighteen-yard line. When Yardley lined up it was seen that Hadlock, at left guard, had been replaced by Ridge. Alf called on Roeder and that dependable young gentleman made five yards. Tom secured four more and Alf punted to Dowling in the center of the field. The Green's quarter back was brought to earth by Ridge. Then Broadwood for the first time made her distance by rushing, Rhodes taking the pigskin for seven yards and then five through center, Mills making the hole for him superbly. Ayres failed to gain on the next try to the disappointment of Broadwood's friends on the side line, and Rhodes tried again. But the ball was Yardley's on downs after the whistle had blown. Then followed a punting dual between Alf and Weldon, the ball sailing back and forth between the two thirty-yard lines. After the fifth exchange the pigskin went to Broadwood on her thirty yards. Then Broadwood hopes revived and Gerald had cause to recall Arthur's prophecy that Broadwood would "come back hard." The Green's full back made first down in two plunges at the Blue's line and then Ayres ran ten yards around left end. Broadwood was cheering like mad now. Ayres was given the pigskin again, but in three attempts at the Yardley line netted but eight yards and the ball went to the Blue.

Sommers was pushed and pulled through left guard for four yards and a penalty gave Yardley five more. Then Roeder made ten yards in two fine rushes, and Alf's forward pass was carried out in good shape by Dan for a long gain but was called back. Alf then punted to Ayres and Weldon returned the kick to Alf, and the latter was thrown on his twenty-yard line. Roeder by this time was pretty well played out and Stearns was substituted, Roeder receiving the biggest kind of an ovation as he walked uncertainly off the field.

Stearns was given the ball on the first play and negotiated three yards at right tackle. Sommers got five at left guard and Alf punted to Ayres on Broadwood's fifty-one yards. Weldon returned the compliment and Alf made a soul-stirring running catch of the punt on his twenty-five-yard line. Tom and Stearns made nine yards between them and Tom secured first down on a split play that caught Broadwood napping. Yardley seemed now to have found her pace, for Stearns and Sommers twice made first down, and Broadwood's line appeared to be weakening. But the gain went for little, since, on the next play, Yardley was put back fifteen yards for holding. The ball was now on Yardley's forty-seven-yard line. Alf tried a forward pass to Dan, who fumbled the ball but recovered it on the enemy's forty yards, while the blue flags waved joyously and the Yardley cheers broke forth again. Stearns made a gain twice, and Alf once more tried a forward pass. Dickenson secured it and made twelve yards before he was stopped. The pigskin was down on Broadwood's twenty-three yards now and Broadwood supporters were imploring their team to "Hold them! Hold them! Hold them!"

Tom made six yards past Mills and Stearns failed to gain. The ball was on the Green's fifteen yards and pandemonium reigned about the field. Broadwood and Yardley shouts and cheers met and mingled in a meaningless jumble of sound. Another forward pass, Alf to Dan, and the two teams, desperate, panting, determined, stood on the seven-yard line. Stearns made two and Tom two more and the ball was three scant yards from the line. And then, amid such an uproar as Broadwood field had seldom heard, Tom crashed through right tackle for a touchdown.

That was too much for the Yardley adherents. Over and under the rope they streamed out onto the field, while caps and flags sailed in air and everyone shouted to his heart's content. The ensuing two minutes were occupied in clearing the field, and as Yardley's rejoicing died down the Broadwood cheer made itself heard. Then Coke kicked goal without trouble and again the blue flags waved. The teams changed goals and Mills kicked off, but four minutes later the whistle blew with Yardley in possession of the ball on her thirty-seven-yard line. The rival elevens cheered each other breathlessly and started for the gymnasium as the Yardley fellows streamed onto the field. One by one the members of the Blue team were captured and borne off in triumph on the shoulders of their joyous companions, while Broadwood cheered her defeated warriors and sang her songs. As Paul Rand and Goodyear and another chap set Alf on his feet at the entrance to the gymnasium Captain Mills came up. His face was white and tired and drawn, but at sight of Alf a smile lighted it up and he turned with outstretched hand.

"It was your day, Loring," he said heartily. "My congratulations."

"Sorry we couldn't both win, Mills," replied Alf, as he shook hands. "Your men played a great game."

Mills smiled and nodded and passed on into the building.

"Poor chap!" thought Alf, in genuine sympathy. "I wonder if I could have smiled like that if we'd lost. He's a dandy, big-hearted fellow, that Mills."

CHAPTER XIV
AROUND THE BONFIRE

Well, Yardley had cause for rejoicing that day, and rejoice she did; she rejoiced all the way back to Wissining; she rejoiced all during supper and she continued to rejoice until long after she should have been in bed and asleep. It isn't often that a school has two victories over her dearest rival in one day to celebrate, and Yardley realized the fact and made the most of the privilege. Supper was a noisy, riotous event, with Mr. Collins striving hard to maintain some degree of order without unnecessarily dampening the enthusiasm with which he was thoroughly in sympathy. Commons was cleared early in order that the team might hold its banquet. But, although driven from the dining room, the fellows didn't go farther than the corridor, and when the members of the team appeared, one by one, they had to literally fight their way to the door through a seething throng of shouting enthusiasts. When they were all inside, players and substitutes, coachers and managers, and Andy Ryan, the doors were closed and locked, and after a final cheer that seemed to shake the very foundations of Whitson, the fellows piled out of the building, formed into procession and, shouting and singing, proceeded to follow a long-established custom and visit the faculty. From building to building they went and one after another the professors and instructors showed themselves at the windows of their rooms, or appeared at the doorways and made their little speeches of congratulation and were cheered. Even Mrs. Ponder, the matron, had to show herself and bow, while "Mr. McCarthy," the janitor, got a full-sized cheer as the procession passed his lodgings in the basement of Oxford. Finally it was Dr. Hewitt's turn and the fellows massed outside his windows and demanded audience. Presently the curtain went up in his study and the doctor raised the window.

"Rah, rah, rah, Hewitt!" was the greeting. The principal bowed and smiled and held up his hand for silence. "Old Toby," as he was called, was getting well along in years and his voice didn't travel very far.

"Young gentlemen," he said, "I am very glad to learn of your victory——"

"Two of them, doctor!" sung out an irrepressible youth at the back of the crowd.

"And glad to learn that the contest passed without injury to any of the players of either side and without regrettable incidents of any sort. The game of football, as you all know, is being much criticised these days and I wish to remind you that it is only by fair and gentlemanly methods of play that you can—ah—appease such criticism. I congratulate you heartily, and thank you. Good night."

The doctor bowed again and disappeared to the accompaniment of a hearty cheer. Then the procession passed around to the front entrance of Oxford and broke ranks to await the appearance of the team. Joe Chambers, who had been appointed chief marshal of the evening's proceedings, dispatched a messenger to the banquet to learn what progress was being made. He was back in a jiffy with the report that they were only half through, and Chambers addressed the meeting.

"Fellows, the team is only about halfway through dinner. After dinner they will elect a captain and that will take some time. I don't believe they'll be ready for an hour yet. Suppose we march down to the field now and get the bonfire started. Then when the team are ready they'll join us there."

"Bonfire! Bonfire! On to the field! Fall in there!"

So the procession formed again and marched down to the field where material for the fire had already been assembled. There were half a dozen nice kerosene barrels and plenty of wood gathered along the river. There were also some railroad ties, a portion of a foot bridge and a section of picket fence which, I fear, had not been so innocently procured. Willing hands massed the barrels and piled the miscellaneous material on top of the pyramid. Then Chambers applied the match and the flames leaped up.

"Ring! Ring!" was the cry. "Form a ring! Everyone join hands!"

In a minute some two hundred and forty rollicking youths were swinging around the fire in a huge circle, advancing, retreating, winding and twisting like a snake that had swallowed its tail, while to the starlit sky two hundred and forty voices arose in song.

> "Oh, the wearin' o' the Green!
> Oh, the wearin' o' the Green!
> You can always tell a loser by the wearin' o' the Green!
> 'Twas the most distressful ruction that ever yet was seen
> When we walloped poor old Broadwood for the wearin' o' the Green!"

They sang it over and over, keeping time to their steps. Then the ring began to move faster and faster until at last it was whirling around the fire like a mammoth pin wheel, the long shadows of the leaping figures waving and dancing grotesquely behind them. The ring broke and met again, fellows fell and were dragged along willy-nilly until they found their feet, and all the time the white stars were informed that:

"You can always tell a loser by the wearin' o' the Green!"

Finally, tired and breathless, the fellows ceased their dancing, the fire was replenished and speeches were demanded. Joe Chambers was elevated to the shoulders of three of his comrades, and when he had found his breath told them that the day would live forever in the annals of Yardley Hall School, and the names of the heroes who had won glory for the Blue on the trampled field of battle would be for all time emblazoned upon the tablets of memory. Joe let himself out to the full limit of his oratorical powers and the audience laughed and cheered and called for more whenever he threatened to slip from his precarious seat or ran out of breath. And just when he was showing signs of real exhaustion the cry went up that the team was coming, and Joe was deposited unceremoniously on the ground while a great shout of welcome went up as the group of players and coaches came out of the darkness into the circle of the fire light.

"Who's captain?" cried a small prep. But he was promptly sat upon, for it is the retiring captain's privilege to announce the result of the election.

"This way!" shouted Joe Chambers. "Everyone over to the grand stand!" So everyone scuttled across the field, the members of the football team being caught up in the stampede as they hustled along.

The light from the fire illumined the faces of the players dimly as they climbed the stand and stood somewhat sheepishly awaiting proceedings. The cheering came first, with Joe leading:

"Now, fellows, a regular cheer for Captain Loring, and make it good!"

Then: "Now, fellows, a regular cheer for Mr. Payson!"

Then: "A short cheer for Dickenson!"

And so it went, every player receiving his applause. Finally they cheered for Mr. Rogers, the assistant coach, for the management and for Andy Ryan, ending up in a long nine-times-three for Yardley. Then there was a call for "Loring! Loring! Speech!" Alf stepped to the front of the stand.

"Fellows, there isn't much to say, I guess," he began earnestly. "But I do want to thank you all for the way you've stood behind the team this year. You've been great to us. We spoke of that at dinner to-night, and every fellow on the team or connected with it agreed that the support you have given us has helped more than you know. We had our troubles in the middle of the season, but you didn't lose faith in us because we were defeated. You kept up our courage, and to-day, when we went onto the field at Broadwood, everyone of us knew that you were right back of us. And that knowledge helped us to win."

"A-a-ay!" murmured the audience.

"Now that the game is over," Alf went on, "I'll say frankly that few of us expected to win it. I didn't, Mr. Payson didn't. But we knew *you* expected us to, and you saw the way the fellows played. I'm proud of having captained such a team. There wasn't a man on it who didn't work every minute from the first of the season until the final whistle this afternoon with just the one end in view of beating Broadwood. We've pulled together all the fall. Not a man has shirked, and the work wasn't easy sometimes, either. I want to tell you that you had a mighty fine team this year!"

Loud agreement from the throng below.

Winning His "Y": A Story of School Athletics

"Now, as to next year. You'll have the start of a good team, for only six of the fellows who started the game to-day graduate this spring. Then there's a lot of good material on the Second team. And right here I want to thank the members of the Second for the way in which they worked with us. They got more hard knocks than glory, and they deserve a whole lot of praise. So, next year I don't see any reason why you can't have another celebration like this. There are some of us up here who won't be on hand to see it, but we all wish you success, and you may be pretty sure that when the day of the Broadwood game comes none of us will be very far from a bulletin board. Now, I know you want to hear who it is that is to lead next year's football team to victory. We have chosen him, and we did it on the first ballot. He's a fellow who has fairly won the honor, not only on account of his playing both last year and this, but because on a certain occasion last fall, when certain defeat at the hands of Broadwood stared us in the face, he endeared himself to us all by an act of self-sacrifice that was finer than all the touchdowns ever made. Fellows, I call for a regular cheer for Captain Vinton!"

CHAPTER XV
THE NEW CAPTAIN MAKES A SPEECH

That *was* a cheer! They might almost have heard it at Broadwood! "*Rah, rah, rah! Rah, rah, rah! Rah, rah, rah! Vinton!*" And after the cheer every fellow shouted his applause in the way that best pleased him and the demonstration threatened to last all night. But some one began to demand "Speech! Speech! Vinton! Vinton!" and poor Dan was thrust into the speaker's place and the tumult died abruptly.

"Fellows," began Dan in a low voice.

"Louder!" called those at the edge of the throng. Dan cleared his throat, smiled nervously and started again.

"Fellows, I thank you very much. I never made a speech and so I don't know how. I——"

"You're doing fine!" called some one reassuringly, and in the laughter that ensued Dan gained courage.

"When they were good enough to elect me awhile ago the only thing that—that made me hesitate about accepting the honor was the thought that if I did I might have to make a speech! I asked Alf—Captain Loring—and he said that maybe I could get out of it. I—the only thing I have to say is that I'm mighty proud to be captain and I'll do the best I can. And—and thank you all. Now let's have a cheer for Loring!"

And Dan, with a sigh of relief, stepped back as Chambers led the cheering. After that Payson said a few words, and then the procession formed again, marched once around the bonfire, singing "The Wearin' o' the Green," and went back up the slope to Oxford, where, massed in front of the steps, the fellows, with bare heads, sang "The Years Roll On."

> "The years roll on. Too soon we find
>   Our boyhood days are o'er.
> The scenes we've known, the friends we've loved
>   Are gone to come no more.
> But in the shrine of Memory

> We'll hold and cherish still
> The recollection fond of those
> Dear days on Yardley Hill.
>
> "The years roll on. To man's estate
> From youthful mold we pass,
> And life's stern duties bind us round,
> And doubts and cares harass.
> But God will guard through storms and give
> The strength to do his will
> And treasure e'er the lessons learned
> Of old on Yardley Hill."

After that, although many of the fellows still lingered about the front of Oxford, the celebration was over with. It was late and most everyone was tired after what had been a busy and exciting day. Also, November nights are chilly in the neighborhood of Wissining and there was an icy little breeze blowing in from the sound. So it wasn't long before the last fellow had sought the warmth and light of his room, leaving the white stars alone to look down on the flickering remains of the fire.

Dan was silent as he climbed the stairs of Clarke and sought No. 28. To be sure, he went up alone, after saying good night to Alf and Tom and Joe Chambers and several others at the corner of the building, and that might explain it if it were not for the fact that Dan usually either sang or whistled as he ran upstairs. To-night he didn't even run. He was much too tired and sore. He had played a hard game for all there was in it and he had received his full share of knocks and bruises. There were no scars visible, but he knew where he could put his hand on a dandy lump! The fact that he limped a little with his right leg indicated in a general way the location of the lump. Besides that, there were plenty of bruised places, and he had an idea that by to-morrow he would be an interesting study in black and blue. When he opened the door of the room he found Gerald there before him, Gerald sitting on the edge of his bed partly undressed and looking very forlorn and a trifle red about the eyes.

"Hello, Gerald," exclaimed Dan. "What's the trouble?"

"Nothing," answered Gerald, diligently hunting on the floor for a stocking which was draped gracefully over his knee. Dan went over and seated himself beside him on the bed.

"Something's up, chum," he said kindly, putting an arm over the younger boy's shoulders. "Let's hear about it."

"It—it isn't anything," replied Gerald with the suspicion of a sniff. "I guess I'm just sort of tired."

"I should think you might be," said Dan heartily, "after the work you did this morning! You made a great hit with the school, Gerald. If it hadn't been for you we'd have lost that race as sure as shooting!"

"That's just it," said Gerald, after a moment, aggrievedly.

"What's just it? You aren't downhearted because you ran a bully race and won the meet, are you?"

"No, but—but other fellows when they win points for the school get—get recognition!"

"Recognition? Great Scott, chum, the fellows cheered you until they were hoarse! Didn't you know that?"

"I—I didn't hear much of it, but Arthur said they did."

"They certainly did! Why, I've heard lots and lots of fellows say how plucky you were and how glad they were that you beat Jake Hiltz."

"But I don't get my Y," said Gerald. "When other fellows do anything they get their Y or they get their numerals or—or something."

"But none of the Cross-Country Team get a Y," exclaimed Dan.

"I don't see why they shouldn't, though," Gerald mourned. "Do you?"

"N-no, I don't," Dan acknowledged. "I guess next year they'll change that. You see, chum, it's a new sport here and it isn't exactly recognized yet."

"It's just as hard work as playing basket ball," said Gerald, "and if you play basket ball you get your two B's."

"Why don't you mention it to Maury? He's your captain, isn't he?" Gerald nodded. "He might see Bendix about it. I think myself that you fellows ought to get something in the way of letters. As you say, it's just as important as basket ball."

"I thought perhaps I'd get my Y," said Gerald.

"And you were disappointed, eh? Is that it? Well, cheer up. You'll get your Y soon enough. You want to remember that as it is now you can only get it in football, baseball, track or hockey."

"Could I get it in hockey?" asked Gerald eagerly.

"Yes, if you made the team and played against Broadwood," replied Dan with a smile. "But you're rather young yet to talk about getting your Y, Gerald."

"I'm fifteen. Stevenson is not much older and he has his. He got it on the track team."

"He's the fellow that jumps, isn't he?"

"He hurdles."

"Well, Stevenson is at least a year older than you are, chum. I tell you what, though; you ought to be able to get your C this winter if you make the dormitory hockey team."

"I don't want a dormitory letter," said Gerald. "I want to get something worth while. I'm going to ask Alf if he will let me on the hockey team."

"He will let you on without being asked if you show that you deserve a place," said Dan soberly. "But don't try to swipe, Gerald." Gerald looked a bit sulky for a minute, but he made no answer. "I don't see, though," Dan continued, "why you shouldn't try for the hockey team. You're a mighty good skater and you seem to know how to handle a stick pretty well, although I'm not much of a judge. The only thing against you is that you're pretty light."

"Well, I'm going to try, anyhow," said Gerald more cheerfully. "Are you?"

Winning His "Y": A Story of School Athletics

"I don't know. I promised Alf last year that I would, and he says he's going to hold me to it. But I'm a poor skater and what I don't know about hockey would fill a book, and a pretty big one."

"I wish you would," said Gerald. "When do they start practice?"

"Oh, some time in December; about the middle, I think. But there isn't usually much doing until after Christmas vacation. I suppose it's a question of ice. Alf's got a scheme of flooding that bit of meadow near the river just this side of the boat house and having the rink there. He says the trouble with playing on the river is that the ice is always cracking. Well, I'm going to bed. You'd better, too, Gerald."

"All right," replied Gerald, coming out of his dreaming. "I'm awfully glad they made you captain, Dan. But I knew they would."

"Did you? That's more than I knew," laughed Dan, as he pulled the bed clothes up and stretched his aching limbs. "I thought it might be Roeder. He deserved it."

"No more than you," asserted Gerald stoutly. "Not as much. Look what you did last year!"

"Well, what interests me now is next year. The fact is, chum, I'm in rather a funk about it. I never realized until to-night what a feeling of responsibility goes with the captaincy. I almost wish that Roeder had got it!"

"I don't. You'll make a bully captain, Dan. Everyone likes you, you're a dandy player and you know how to boss folks. Do you suppose Muscles will let me play next year?"

"Oh, I guess so."

"He ought to. I'll be sixteen then, and in the second class. Do you think I'd stand any show of making it, Dan?"

"You go to sleep. Sufficient unto the day is the football thereof. Good night, Gerald. I'm dead tired."

"Good night," answered Gerald. After a pause he added: "You don't have to be very heavy to play quarter, do you?"

"Not very, I guess. Thinking of quarter?"

"Yes. I've—I've been sort of watching Alf and I think I could play quarter, Dan."

"What?" asked Dan drowsily. "Oh, well, cut out the conversation, Gerald, and take a fall out of Morpheus. Gee, but this old bed feels good!"

Two days later, on Monday the twenty-third, Cambridge and Oxford held their elections and Gerald went through with flying colors and became a member of Cambridge, with the right to wear the Light Blue in the shape of button or hat ribbon. Hiltz accepted what couldn't be helped with apparent good grace. He and Gerald always managed to be looking the other way when they met and they had not spoken since the cross-country meet. Hiltz also avoided Dan, since he had not forgiven the latter for beating him at election, but they nodded or spoke when they met. Arthur, too, was in Hiltz's bad books, for Arthur had never made any secret of his assistance to Dan. But neither Dan nor Arthur nor Gerald was troubled about it.

"We're not very popular with Jake nowadays," observed Arthur one evening in Cambridge as Hiltz entered and passed without apparently discovering the presence of Arthur and Dan. "I'll bet he will make trouble for Gerald before the year is over."

"I don't just see how he could," said Dan, "although I don't doubt that he would like to. The fellows are rather tired of Hiltz, I think."

"Maybe, but he isn't tired of himself so that you can notice it. And he thinks he has a grievance. We'll have trouble with him yet, or I miss my guess, Dan."

Dan yawned frankly.

"Well, I guess we can attend to him when the time comes," he said indifferently. "He's most all bluff."

Thanksgiving Day dawned clear and crisp. Dan, Alf and Tom were to dine with Mr. Pennimore and Gerald at Sound View in the evening and so they had decided to cut out the Thanksgiving dinner at school in the middle of the day.

"We won't be able to do justice to Gerald's party if we fill up on turkey at two o'clock," declared Alf. "I tell you what, Dan; let the four of us get some grub and have a picnic." Tom groaned, but Gerald hailed the proposition with delight. Dan looked doubtful.

"Rather chilly, isn't it, for picnics?" he asked, looking out of the window at the breezy landscape.

"No, that's where the fun comes in," answered Alf. "We'll wear sweaters and take some rugs. Then we'll build a dandy big fire — —"

"Where's this going to be?" inquired Tom from where he was stretched out on the window seat with a magazine in his hands.

"Up the river somewhere. We'll take a couple of canoes — —"

"You're always suggesting schemes that demand physical exertion," protested his roommate. "Why don't you ever think up something easy? Why not stay just where we are and have a good, sensible time? It's warm here and I'm quite comfortable."

"What do you say, Dan?" asked Alf, turning his back on Tom and his objections.

"I'm game," said Dan. "I love these pleasure exertions. How about you, Gerald?"

"I'd love to go. It seems a shame to stay around school when we have a holiday. What time would we get back? You know we're going for an automobile ride at four."

"That's something I like," said Tom approvingly. "That's my idea of pleasure—just as long as I don't have to blow up any tires."

"We'd be back by three, easy," declared Alf. "What time is it now? Twenty of eleven? Come on then, fellows. I'll go down and see what I can get in the kitchen. You find those football rugs, Tom, and the rest of you hustle into your sweaters. We'll meet at the boat house in a quarter of an hour."

"In that case," murmured Tom, "I have ten minutes more of comfort."

"I'll have to telephone my father," said Gerald. "He doesn't want me to go canoeing, you know, after what happened last spring."

"That's so," said Dan. "You tell him you're going in my canoe, Gerald, and I guess he will let you go."

Winning His "Y": A Story of School Athletics

So the three hurried off, leaving Tom to settle himself more comfortably on the cushions and take up his magazine again with a sigh.

CHAPTER XVI
THE PICNIC

At eleven they were paddling up the river against a stiff tide with the wind quartering the canoes from across the marshes. There was a big pasteboard box of luncheon in Alf and Tom's craft, while between Dan and Gerald lay a pile of rugs. Paddling was rather hard work and, although they started off merrily enough, they soon relapsed into silence and saved their breath for their labor. Once past Flat Island it was easier going, for the stream narrows there and the banks are higher and afford more protection from the wind. Half a mile farther Tom protested.

"Isn't this far enough?" he asked. "What's the good of killing ourselves."

"There isn't a decent place to camp here," answered Alf. "Let's go up where we can find some trees to break the wind. It isn't much farther." Tom groaned and bent over his paddle again. Gerald had learned paddling the year before and was quite an adept, but his softer muscles soon tired and he was heartily glad when Alf finally called a halt, about a mile and a half from school.

"Here's a dandy place," Alf announced, "over here on the left."

"The other side looks better," said Tom.

"No, because over here we'll have the trees between us and the wind. Push her in here, Tom."

The canoes were nosed up on a yard-wide beach of soft sand and the boys disembarked. The bank was only two or three feet high and they scrambled up it, bearing the provisions and rugs. There was a little plateau of grass here and back of it the land sloped up in a tiny ridge thickly grown with young oaks and stunted, misshapen cedars. The fringe of trees broke to some extent the wind, which blew strongly here across a mile of marsh and meadow. There were no houses near, although farther up stream and on the other side a farm was in sight a half mile distant. There was plenty of wood lying along the bank and Dan discovered dead cedar which he uprooted and added to the fuel pile. Alf found a piece of dry pine wood and splintered it with his knife.

"Who's got a piece of paper?" he asked.

"You don't need paper," said Tom. "Use dry grass."

So Alf gathered a few handfuls, leaned his whittlings neatly upon it, set some larger pieces on that and felt in his pockets.

"Got a match, Tom?" he inquired.

Tom went through his clothes and shook his head. Dan followed his example and shook his head likewise. Alf began to look anxious.

"Got a match, Gerald?" he cried. Gerald, who was gathering wood at a little distance, answered promptly and cheerfully.

"No, I haven't, Alf. Will this be enough wood?"

There was no reply for a moment. Then Alf answered dryly: "I think so, Gerald. Yes, I think we have all the wood we can burn—without a match!"

Dan looked about him, his gaze traveling over the landscape. Tom grinned.

"Looking for a match factory, Dan?" he asked pleasantly.

Alf, sitting on his feet, looked ruefully at his neatly arranged pile of grass and splinters and wood. Gerald came up cheerfully with an armful of broken branches.

"There," he said, "that's surely enough. There's a big old log down there, though, if we need it. It was too heavy for me to carry. What—what's the matter?" He stared wonderingly from one to another of the silent trio.

"Nothing to speak of," answered Dan. "Only we haven't any matches."

"It's a mere detail, of course," murmured Tom carelessly.

"Oh!" said Gerald blankly.

"Thank you," said Alf. "It's a remark I've been trying to think of for some time. It—it does full justice to the situation."

"Let's look again," suggested Dan, probing his pockets. Everyone followed suit, but, although a great variety of articles were discovered, no one found a match.

"We're a parcel of idiots," remarked Alf earnestly.

"'We?'" asked Tom in surprise. "No one told me to bring any matches. If they had I'd have brought them. Why, the table was just strewn with them. I noticed them as I left the room."

"It's a wonder you wouldn't put a few in your pocket," replied Alf disgustedly.

"I thought you were attending to the arrangements," said Tom unruffledly. "Well, I shall wrap myself in a rug and go to sleep. I just love these al fresco affairs. I could die picnicking—probably of pneumonia!"

"It is fun, isn't it?" laughed Dan.

"Absolutely matchless," replied Tom cheerfully.

Alf sniffed disgustedly.

"As there are only two rugs, Tom, you'll have to take some one in with you," said Dan. "We might go home and have our luncheon in the room."

"Go home after coming all the way up here?" said Alf fretfully. "That would be a silly thing to do!"

"Yes, I'm surprised at you, Mr. Vinton," said Tom severely. "How much better it would be to stay here comfortably and enjoy the dear little breezes that are wandering caressingly down my spine."

"I saw a match somewhere," said Gerald, gazing into space with a deep frown. Tom viewed him in mock alarm.

"It's hunger and exposure," he whispered. "He's raving! He's seeing matches! It's a frightful symptom!"

"What do you mean?" demanded Alf anxiously. "Where did you see a match?"

"Yes," prompted Dan, "tell the ladies and gentlemen where you saw the match. Give all the details, Gerald. What sort of a match was it? Not a football match, I hope?"

Gerald looked at them blankly, trying to remember.

"I—it was *somewhere*."

"Yes, yes! Go on!" cried Tom hoarsely, clutching his hands in an agony of suspense.

"Oh, cut out the comedy!" begged Alf. "What are you talking about, kid?"

"Why, I saw a match somewhere—just now—since we left school," answered Gerald.

"Where?"

"I can't think."

"Look in your pockets again," said Dan.

"I did."

"Well, did it again, then." Gerald obeyed but had to shake his head when the search was over.

"I observe," remarked Tom, as though speaking to himself, "that yonder lies what looks from here to be a perfectly good farmhouse. I presume that there are matches there and that we might be able to borrow one or two of the priceless things."

"It's a half-mile paddle and a half-mile walk after that," said Alf dejectedly. "Still, you might try it." Tom looked pained and surprised.

"Oh, I wasn't thinking of trying it," he assured them. "I'm not what you'd call an accomplished canoeist, Alf. I haven't your skill, you know."

"Well, I'm not going away up there all alone," said Alf positively. "The wind's too strong. If one of you fellows will go with me——"

"I know!" cried Gerald. He turned and sprang toward the bank, the others following. He clambered into the nearest canoe and began to peer about. Then he went to the second and repeated the operation and in a moment exhibited what at a few yards away had all the earmarks of a match.

"Hooray!" cried Dan. "Is it a good one?"

Gerald viewed it dubiously as he clambered back.

"I—I think so," he answered, handing it over for their inspection. Dan examined it and passed it to Alf, and Alf, with a shake of his head, presented it to Tom. It was about two thirds of a sulphur match and had evidently been exposed, if not to rain, at least to dampness, for the head had lost its brilliancy of hue.

"A most dissipated looking article," pondered Tom. "It looks to me like a match with a sad and eventful past. However"—he returned it to Alf—"see what you can do with it."

"You light it, Dan," said Alf carelessly. But Dan shook his head.

"It would go out as sure as Fate if I tried it. You do it, Tom."

"Never! I decline to assume the terrible responsibility. Let Gerald perform the mystic rite." But Gerald drew back as though Dan were offering him poison.

"I wouldn't dare!" he laughed. "Alf, you do it."

"Well, maybe it won't light, anyway," said Alf, accepting the match and the responsibility. He looked about him. "There's no use trying to light it here in this wind, though."

"Tom and I'll hold one of the rugs up," said Dan.

"All right. But I've got to have a piece of paper. That old grass may not light." Finally Tom sacrificed a half sheet of a letter and the boys gathered anxiously about the little pile of wood and grass, into which Alf had thrust the twisted piece of paper. Tom and Dan held one of the rugs out to form a screen and Alf knelt down and seized the match firmly.

"Wait!" cried Gerald. Alf jumped and dropped the match.

"What's the matter?" he asked crossly, as he recovered the precious article.

"Don't scratch it on your trousers," begged Gerald. "It's old and the brimstone might come off. Scratch it on a rock."

"That's right," commended Dan. "Get a rock, Gerald."

So Gerald found one and laid it beside the pile and once more they all held their breath while Alf, with grim determination writ large upon his countenance, drew the match lightly across the stone. There was an anxious moment, for at first there was no flame to be seen. But then the paper blackened at the edge and little yellow tongues began to lick at the dry grass. Four sighs of relief burst simultaneously upon the air.

"Don't take the rug away yet," begged Alf, as he watched anxiously with his nose some six inches from the fire. Gerald stood ready with more fuel.

"Here's a fine piece of soft pine," he whispered. Alf accepted it silently without taking his watchful gaze from the fire and gingerly added it to the pile. Another piece followed, and another. And then, very cautiously, Alf arose, waved aside the rug and smiled beatifically upon his work.

"There!" he said.

Tom and Dan shook hands in much the manner in which two Arctic explorers might congratulate each other at the North Pole. Alf viewed them disgustedly.

"I'd like to know what you chaps are grinning about. Who made this fire?"

"You applied the match," replied Tom kindly, "but without our skillful and well-performed labor there'd have been no fire. We are the real heroes of the—the conflagration."

As the flames leaped up, crackling merrily, life looked a good deal more cheerful. They piled on dead branches and driftwood until they were forced to move away to a respectful distance. Then they stood and warmed themselves in the grateful heat. Afterwards they spread the rugs on the ground and Alf opened the luncheon box. It was only half past twelve, but their labors and the keen wind had made them hungry. Gerald filled the two tumblers with water from the river and Alf spread out the repast. There was cold roast beef, crackers, plenty of bread ready sliced, butter, salt, currant jelly, cake, some chow-chow pickles which had leaked out of a jelly glass and got into everything, including the salt and cake, and four large rosy apples.

"'Don't take the rug away yet,' begged Alf."

"Gee!" said Tom, "you must have made love to the cook, Alf."

"No," replied his roommate, who had recovered his spirits, "no, it was just my manly beauty and irresistible attraction. Let's toast some of the bread, fellows."

So Alf cut a long branch and sharpened one end and then sat crosslegged as near the flames as he could get with a slice of bread impaled on the end of the improvised toasting fork. It was warm work, but the others encouraged him from time to time, and he stuck it out until he had three slices toasted.

"That first piece is mine," he finally announced. "And if anyone wants any more he'll have to toast it himself."

"I don't want any more, do you, Tom?" asked Dan.

"No, I don't think so," was the cheerful response. Alf looked around suspiciously.

"Here! You've eaten my piece, you cheats!"

"I didn't see any name on the piece I had," Tom assured him.

"Neither did I," said Dan. "Are you sure it was marked, Alf?"

"You go to the dickens!" grumbled Alf, as he retired from the fire very red of face and moist of eye. "I'll give you half of this, Gerald."

"No, I'll toast some," replied Gerald. He took up the stick, produced his knife and sharpened the other end as well. Then he put a piece of bread on one end and stuck the other in the ground at such a slant that the bread was over the hot coals. Then he resumed his seat on the rug.

"What do you think of that!" marveled Tom. "Isn't he the brainy little Solomon? I suppose your boxing lessons taught you how to do that, Gerald."

"Oh, you dry up," said Alf. "And don't eat quite all the cold meat, *if* you please. Where's the chow-chow got to?"

"About everywhere," answered Dan. "I've no doubt the river's yellow with it. Here's what's left, though."

Alf viewed it disgustedly.

"It's a wonder you wouldn't eat all the lunch, you chaps, while I work for you and singe my eyebrows off. Your toast's burning, Gerald."

There wasn't a respectable crumb left when they had finished the repast. They built the fire up again and lolled back on the rugs and talked lazily while the sun traveled westward and the wind whistled through the trees and sent the smoke eddying across the river. They talked the football season all over and played the Broadwood game again from start to finish. And then Tom took up the subject of basket ball and outlined his plans for the season, for he was captain of the Five. Afterwards the talk went on to hockey.

"You're coming out this year," said Alf to Dan. "Don't forget that."

"But I can't skate for a hang," Dan objected.

"You'll pick it up all right. Besides, you could try for goal. We need a good goal tend and you wouldn't have to do much skating there."

"Are you going to play, Tom?" asked Dan. Tom shook his head.

"No, I won't have time."

"Here's one candidate, though," said Dan. "Gerald says he's going out for the team, Alf."

"Good for you, kid!" replied Alf. "The more the merrier."

"But do you think I'll have any show?" asked Gerald eagerly.

"Why, I don't know. Can you skate pretty well?"

"Yes, I think so."

"He's a very good skater," said Dan. "Don't lie, Gerald."

"Well, you come out, anyway," said Alf, "and we'll see what happens. Meanwhile I think we'd better be getting back if the car is to be there at four. It's almost three now!"

"Thank goodness we don't have to paddle back," muttered Tom as he arose and stretched himself. "I'll put these glasses in. You fellows bring the rugs. Ought we to put the fire out?"

"No, let it burn out," said Dan lazily. "It can't do any harm."

Tom walked to the bank, stood there a moment and then returned and seated himself again on the rug, the glasses still in his hands.

"What's the row?" asked Alf, catching sight of Tom's face.

"I was just thinking," replied Tom gravely, "how often we say things without thoroughly realizing the deep significance of them. I made the remark, quite casually, a moment ago that we wouldn't have to paddle back."

"Well?" demanded Alf sharply, propping himself up on his elbow.

"Well, we won't."

"Of course we won't! The current will take us down, you idiot."

"Oh, I see. It will be rather wet, though, won't it?"

"Wet? What are you driving at, Tom?" Dan demanded.

"Me? Nothing at all. If you fellows can stand it I guess I can. But floating down the river in this weather sounds sort of wet and chilly."

"In the canoes?" inquired Alf uneasily.

"Oh, you meant in the canoes? Well, I don't think we'll go in the canoes."

"Why not?"

"There aren't any," said Tom.

CHAPTER XVII
THE RETURN

"What!"

Dan and Alf and Gerald leaped to their feet and ran to the bank. Then they looked at each other in blank dismay. Below them the wet sand still showed where the canoes had rested, but the canoes themselves had utterly vanished. Tom sauntered up, his hands in his pockets, whistling softly.

"It really is a beautiful view from here," he murmured. Alf turned on him irritably.

"Tom, don't be an absolute fool, will you?" he begged.

"That's right, cut out the humor for a minute," Dan agreed. "There isn't anything especially funny about having to walk all the way home!"

"Thought we were going to float," said Tom with a grin. They turned from him in impatient disgust, Alf muttering things uncomplimentary to his friend's mental condition.

"I don't see—" began Dan.

"Oh, it's plain enough," Alf cut in. "They weren't drawn up very far and when Gerald got in them he pushed them off a little and the wind did the rest. They're probably out in the sound by this time."

"I'm awfully sorry," said Gerald humbly.

"Oh, it wasn't your fault," answered Alf. "We ought to have drawn them up farther. I never thought about the wind."

"Nor I," said Dan.

"If you'd taken my advice and camped on the other side," observed Tom sweetly, "this wouldn't have happened."

"You be blowed! But, see here, Alf; the wind may have blown them ashore on the other bank lower down."

"Wouldn't help us much," replied Alf. "But we might go down a ways and see if we can find them."

"If we do find them I'll swim over and get them," said Dan, as they went along the bank.

"Indeed you won't! You'd catch cold a day like this. But I would like to be sure that they haven't gone sailing out to sea."

They went on silently and dejectedly for nearly a quarter of a mile. There their farther progress was barred by a small stream which flowed into the river from the marsh.

"We might get across this by wading," said Dan, "but there are any number more of them."

The canoes were not in sight, although from where they had halted they could see both banks of the river as far as the next turn, an eighth of a mile below.

"Well, what's to be done?" asked Alf.

"Walk home," answered Dan. "It's about six miles, though, the way we'll have to go, for we'll have to make a circle around the marsh and hit the Broadwood road somewhere beyond the Cider Mill. Even so, we're in for wet feet."

"If we were only on the other side," mourned Gerald.

"That would be a cinch," said Dan.

"'Over on the Jersey side,'" hummed Tom. "Look here, six miles may appeal to you chaps, but it likes me not."

"Well," inquired Alf belligerently, "what do you propose, Mr. Fixit?"

"I propose, Mr. Grouch, that we walk *up* the river instead of down."

"That's so," agreed Dan. "There's a bridge about a mile and a half up there. That would make it only about four miles and a half to school instead of six."

"And six is a most optimistic calculation of the other route," added Tom. "I'll bet it's nearer seven."

"I don't suppose there's any place in this old stream where we could ford it, is there?" asked Alf, looking wrathfully at the river.

"Guess not. You know we can go in canoes up as far as the old coal wharf, and that's a good four miles above here."

"We might swim it," said Gerald.

"Yes, and get our clothes wet and have pneumonia," responded Alf. "I guess not. Come on, then; we'll foot it to the bridge."

"Well, let's do something. I'm getting frozen." And Dan led the way back along the edge of the river. When they had reached their picnic site they stood for a moment around the dwindling fire and warmed their chilled bodies.

"Let's leave these things here," suggested Tom, "and come up for them to-morrow."

"You can leave your rug if you want to," replied Alf, "but I prefer to take mine along. I don't care to lose it; it cost money."

"That's different, of course," answered Tom cheerfully. "They gave me mine with a pair of suspenders. Nevertheless I cherish it deeply and will e'en bear it with me."

"They may keep us from freezing to death before we get home," said Dan morosely.

"Oh, you won't be cold by the time you reach the bridge," answered Tom. "All ready? Who's got the pesky glasses? You, Gerald? Give them to me and I'll stick 'em in my pockets. That's all right. Now, then, the bridge party will proceed."

It was a rather silent quartet that tramped along the river bank in the wind. Luckily they were leaving the marshes behind, and, although they did get their feet wet more than once, they encountered no streams. The mile and a half seemed nearer three, but that was no doubt due to the fact that they had to stumble through bushes and briars and force their way through thickets.

"Was that one of the school canoes you had?" asked Alf once.

"Yes," Dan replied sadly. "How much will they charge me for it, do you think?"

"About twenty-five, I guess. Maybe it will be found, though."

"Gee, I hope so! You had your own, didn't you?"

"Yes, mine and Tom's. I don't care so much about that, though; I daresay I wouldn't have used it much more, anyway."

"Let it go," said Tom cheerfully. "It has played us false."

"You're a queer dub," said Dan, turning to him with a smile. "Most of the time you don't open your mouth. To-day you're real sort of chatty. Adversity seems to agree with you, Tom."

"Oh, it isn't that," was the reply. "It's the picnic. Picnics always make me bright and sunny. I'm crazy about them and don't know when I've ever enjoyed one more. You—you get so close to Nature, don't you?"

"You surely do," answered Dan, stumbling over a blackberry runner and picking himself up again. "Too close!"

"There's the bridge!" cried Gerald from the end of the procession.

"Praises be!" said Alf. "I only hope it will hold together long enough for us to get across. It looks as though it might tumble down any moment."

"Never look a bridge in the mouth till you come to it," said Tom. "To me it is a most beautiful structure, far, far more beautiful than the Brooklyn Bridge or the Bridge of Sighs or any of the *ponts* of dear old Paris. Don't you love the *ponts* of Paris, Dan?"

"I'm wild about plaster of Paris," laughed Dan as they reached the narrow road and turned onto the old wagon bridge. Once across it they continued along the road instead of following the river back.

"The railroad's only a little way over," said Alf, "and I'm sick of looking at that measly little ditch."

"Remember the rules, Alf," cautioned Tom. "No walking on the railroad, you know."

"Hang the rules! I want to get home!"

"So do I, but not in pieces. I knew a fellow once who was walking on the railroad and a train came up behind him and he didn't get off and—" Tom paused eloquently.

"And cr-r-rushed him, I suppose," Dan inquired.

"No, he was on the other track," answered Tom. "It's always safer to be on the other track. I shall walk on the other track all the way home."

"Tom, you're a perfect idiot to-day," said Alf disgustedly. "You aren't nearly as funny as you think you are."

"And you're not nearly as grouchy as you think you are," replied Tom good-naturedly. "Behold, gentlemen and one other, the railroad, passing, as you see, from thither to yon; also back again on the other track. How do we get down there? Jump?"

"No, fall," said Dan, scrambling down the steep bank. "I want to tell you, though, that I'm going to get out of here before I come in sight of school. Old Toby is daffy about fellows walking on the railroad tracks."

"Hope we don't meet him coming the other way," said Tom. "What would you do if we did, Alf? Just whistle and speed by?"

"No, I'd jump the track and run like the dickens," answered Alf. "I wonder why they don't put these fool ties the same distance apart."

"It's awfully good exercise," said Dan. "How are you getting on, Gerald?"

"All right," Gerald replied a trifle breathlessly. "I thought I heard a whistle then, Dan."

"Old Toby, I'll bet a hat!" cried Tom.

"Well, if a train comes," answered Dan, "don't try to guess which track it's on but get off on one side as quick as you know how and give it plenty of room."

Gerald had a chance to profit by Dan's advice a few minutes later when a local came screeching down on them from the east. The boys drew off at one side of the track and held onto their caps, for the cut was narrow and the engine and cars went by at not much more than arm's length.

"That engine bit at me," gasped Alf when the last car had hurtled by in a blinding cloud of dust and smoke. "Gee, but my eyes are full of cinders!"

"Why didn't you shut them?" asked Tom. "That was a narrow escape, fellows, I tell you. A yard farther that way and we'd have been ground to atoms."

"I guess the next time I'll climb the bank," observed Gerald with a somewhat sickly smile. "I thought that engine was going to reach out and grab me!"

"There probably won't be any next time," said Dan. "Not if we foot it a little faster. What time is it, anyway? By Jupiter, Alf, it's a quarter past four!"

"I'm automobiling this minute," sighed Tom. "Say, did we have any luncheon or did I just dream it? I'm certainly terribly lonesome inside."

"I could eat tacks," said Alf. "Double-pointed ones, too. Let's hit up the pace a bit."

They did, but soon tired, for the ties were never just where they should have been and progress consisted of hops and skips and occasional jumps. Tom voiced the general sentiment when he observed pantingly: "Fellows, this is very tie-some. I shall moderate my transports, if I never get home."

"You mean transportation," suggested Dan.

"I mean that I'm going to walk the rest of the way calmly and with dignity. This thing of being a goat and leaping from crag to crag makes me nervous. Anyway, we're getting pretty near school and I vote that we quit being railroad trains and hit the road."

"Road nothing! Come up this side and go through the woods," said Alf. "It's a heap nearer."

So they climbed a steep bank, shinned over a high fence and left the railroad cut. Ten minutes of devious progress through woods and across fields brought them to the school. Tom subsided on the steps of Clarke.

"I can go no further," he declared. "Bring up the auto, Gerald."

"I'm afraid it's gone home again," said Gerald. "But it isn't too late to take a ride, is it? Just a short one."

"Ride! What is a ride?" demanded Alf. "I've walked so much I can't imagine doing anything else."

"I'll go and telephone home and ask them to send the car back," said Gerald.

"That's the ticket. But, look here, what about dressing? Do we get into our party rags now or after the ride?"

"Afterwards," said Gerald. "We'll come back at six and dinner isn't until seven."

"Good!" said Alf. "I'll just crawl over and eradicate some of the signs of travel; and incidentally get about a quart of cinders out of my eyes. We'll come up to the room in about ten minutes, Dan."

"Right O! I don't think a little exercise with a whisk broom and soap and water would hurt me any, either. What's this?"

"This," answered Tom, "or rather, these, are the glasses, Dan. I appoint you a committee of one to restore them to the kitchen."

"You run away and play! Take them back yourself, you old lazy chump!"

"But I didn't borrow them. They might not like——"

"Neither did I. Give them to Alf."

But Alf had already departed, and with a groan Tom made his way to Whitson, limping pathetically. On the steps he paused and looked back at Dan, who had watched the performance amusedly. Tom raised the hand holding the tumblers high in air.

"Picnic!" he called across. "Never again!"

CHAPTER XVIII
BUILDING THE RINK

There may be better ways of putting one's self in condition to do justice to a Thanksgiving Day dinner than paddling a mile and a half in a canoe, walking five miles after that and finishing up with a forty-mile ride in an automobile. If there are, I can't think of them at this moment. And at all events never, surely, were four hungrier boys ever gathered around a table than the quartet that did full and ample justice to Mr. Pennimore's hospitality that evening. I shan't go into many details regarding that repast, for I don't want to make you envious, but it was an old-fashioned Thanksgiving banquet, with oysters from the host's own oyster beds, a clear soup, celery and olives, a turkey that, as Alf said, would have been an ostrich if it had lived another day or two, a roast ham that fell to pieces under the carving knife, vegetables without end, a salad that held most all the colors of the rainbow and as many flavors, a pumpkin pie looking like a full harvest moon, ice cream and sherbet in the form of turkeys seated on nests of yellow spun sugar, little cakes with all shades of icing, black grapes nearly as big as golf balls from the Sound View conservatories, apples like the pictures in nursery catalogues, oranges, pears, nuts and raisins and candy. And there was all the sweet cider they wanted, and, finally, black coffee and toasted crackers and some cheese that Tom helped himself to lavishly and afterwards viewed with deep suspicion.

It was almost nine when the chairs were pushed back and the diners adjourned to the big crackling fire in the library. Tom lowered himself cautiously into an armchair with a blissful groan.

"I don't believe," he said, "that I shall want to eat again until Christmas. I know now why the Puritans used to go to church in the morning on Thanksgiving Day. They never would have had enough energy to give thanks after dinner!"

Mr. Pennimore led the talk around to subjects nearest to the hearts of his guests and soon had them chattering merrily of school and sports. Tom begged him to come over some time and see a basket ball game.

"I'd like to," said Mr. Pennimore, "but you know I close the house here to-morrow and go back to New York. I hardly think I shall be in Wissining again before spring. I'm sorry I can't see some of your winter sports, Tom."

"You ought to see us lick Broadwood at hockey," said Gerald.

"Hockey? Let me see, we used to call that shinny or shinty when I was a boy, didn't we?"

Alf explained the modern form of the game and they talked over the outlook for the season. "I'm going to get the team together in about a week," he said. "Sometimes we have fairly good ice before Christmas, and when we don't we can get a lot of practice at shooting in the gym. I'm going to try and make a goal out of Dan."

"I'd like to play myself," said Tom, "if Dan's going to be the goal. What's he going to do? Stand and hold his mouth open?"

"I'm going to try for the team, too, sir," said Gerald importantly.

"Are you?" asked his father with a smile. "Well, don't get hurt, son. Ice is hard stuff to fall on, and it seems to me that I recollect getting hit once or twice on the shins with a stick. It was rather painful, I believe."

"It hurts like the dickens," laughed Alf. "And when your hands are cold and some one raps them it feels as though they were busted."

"What do you play for?" asked Mr. Pennimore. "I mean what is the trophy?"

"There isn't any, sir. We just play for the honor. Beating Broadwood is enough in itself."

"Ah, I see. I was going to propose putting a cup up. How would that do?"

"Great!" exclaimed Alf.

"Go ahead, dad!" said Gerald eagerly. "A great big one!"

"Oh, I don't think it's necessary to have it very big, is it, Alf? Suppose I offer a cup to be played for for three years, the team winning twice to take permanent possession. Would that be a good plan?"

"Yes, sir, it would be a dandy idea," answered Alf with enthusiasm. "The team that won it this year could keep it until next. It would be mighty nice of you, sir."

"All right, I'll attend to it when I get to town. I'll have the silversmith make a sketch and send it down for you to pass on. I suppose he will have some ideas on the subject."

"How big would it be, sir?" asked Gerald.

"Oh, I'll leave that to you boys. What do you say, Alf?"

"I should think about eight inches high, sir; a sort of a loving-cup effect."

"They might work in some crossed hockey sticks," Dan suggested, "and the Yardley and Broadwood flags."

"Yes, that's a good idea. I'll remember that. You see what you think of the design that's sent you, Alf, and then write the firm and suggest any changes you like. We'll call it the—what shall we call it?"

"The Pennimore Cup, sir," answered Alf and Tom in chorus.

"Hum; no, I'm not looking for glory. Let's call it the Sound View Cup. How will that do?"

"Pennimore Cup sounds better, sir," said Dan.

"I think so, too," Alf agreed. "Let's call it that, sir."

"All right," laughed their host. "I haven't any objection. The Pennimore Cup it is, then. And I hope you fellows get it for good in the end."

"I hope we get it this year, anyway," said Alf. "I'll get French—he's our manager—to write over and tell Broadwood about it. It ought to please them."

"It'll please them so much," murmured Tom sleepily, "that they'll come over here and carry it home with them."

"If they do it will be after the hardest tussle they ever had," declared Alf. "We're going to have a hockey seven that will be a dandy!"

Winning His "Y": A Story of School Athletics

Dan and Alf and Tom said good night and good-by at ten. Gerald, since his father was to take his departure on the morrow, had obtained permission to spend the night at Sound View. The others shook hands with Mr. Pennimore on the porch and then piled into the automobile and were whisked home, a very tired and sleepy and contented trio. By all the rules and laws of compensation every last one of them ought to have suffered that night with indigestion. But they didn't. Instead, they dropped into sound sleep as soon as their heads touched the pillows and never woke until the sunlight was streaming in at the windows.

The lost canoes were recovered the next day. Alf's was found caught on a snag at the up-stream end of Flat Island, Dan's beached just below the railroad bridge. Some one had evidently seen it and pulled it ashore, thereby earning Dan's deep gratitude.

A few days later the candidates for the hockey team were summoned to a meeting in the gymnasium and Alf outlined the season's plans to them. Faculty had agreed to allow them a schedule of eight games, with the Broadwood contest closing the season on the twentieth of February. The first game, with St. John's, was arranged for January ninth. Alf said he wanted the fellows to put in every moment possible during the Christmas recess on skates.

"Play hockey if you can. If you can't, take a hockey stick with you and learn to use it with both hands. Buy a puck and try shooting, too. Put a couple of sticks or stones on the ice and try to shoot the puck between them. You ought all of you to have a fair idea of hockey by the time you get back to school. We have a few dollars in the treasury already, but we are going to use that to build a rink on the meadow. So every fellow will have to buy his own sticks this year. From now until vacation there will be practice every afternoon but Saturdays in the baseball cage or in the rowing room. Of course, if we get ice we'll go out of doors. You'd better each of you buy a book of rules and study it. You can get the book in Greenburg at Proctor's, and it costs you only ten cents. So don't tell me you can't afford it. Any fellow who thinks that's too much money, however, can go to French and he will buy the book for him. That's all for this time, I guess. Four o'clock Monday next here in the gym."

"Shall we wear skates?" some one inquired.

"You may wear roller skates if you have them," replied Alf, joining in the laughter. "We don't expect to learn to skate indoors, however, simply to use the stick and shoot. By the way, though, there is one more thing. We've got to get the rink ready before the ground freezes. We're going to throw up embankments of earth about a foot high. Mr. McCarthy has agreed to do that for us, but he can only work at it an hour or so a day. Now, suppose to-morrow afternoon we all go down and give him a hand. We'd get it done then and would save money, too; and we need all the money we've got. What do you say?"

What they said was evident from the fact that the next afternoon some thirty boys of various ages and sizes were merrily throwing up the ground with whatever implements they had been able to requisition. Alf and Dan and Dick French had marked off the ground and set stakes, and before dark the rink was ready for the ground to freeze.

"What I don't just comprehend," observed Dan, as they stood in the twilight viewing the result with satisfaction, "is how you propose to get the water in here. The river is about four feet below the level of the rink."

"Pump it, my dear boy. Mr. McCarthy has a hand pump and he will rig it up over there on the bank. Then we'll build a trough effect of boards and run the water into the rink."

"Oh," said Dan, nodding. "When are you going to do that?"

"Just as soon as the ground freezes hard."

"What's that got to do with it?"

"Lots. If the ground isn't frozen the water will seep into it about as fast as we run it on. Comprehend?"

"Yes, your Highness. It's quite simple—when you know it. Now let's go to supper and let it freeze."

"It won't do much freezing this sort of weather," said French. "Smells like snow, doesn't it?"

"I didn't know snow had any smell," said Alf. "What I'd like to do if we could afford it, fellows, is to put planks around the sides."

"How much would it cost?" asked French.

"I don't know. I'll come down to-morrow, though, and see how many planks it would take. They wouldn't need to be more than ten inches broad. We could sink them two inches under the ice and that would leave eight inches above to stop the puck. You can do a lot better if you have something for the puck to carrom off of. I wish we had as good a rink as Broadwood has."

"Maybe another year we can," said French. "If we turn out a good team this winter perhaps the fellows will contribute toward fixing this up."

"Yes, but I won't be here," laughed Alf. "And I find that what is going to happen next year doesn't interest me as much as it ought to!"

With football over, the school settled for awhile into a quiet untroubled by athletic excitement. To be sure hockey and basket ball candidates practiced busily, but there were no matches to distract attention from study, which was an excellent thing for many of the students, since examination had begun to loom large on the horizon. Gerald, whose attention had been greatly distracted of late, was enabled to placate Mr. McIntyre by greatly improving his class standing in mathematics, a subject which held for him more terrors than any other study.

At four o'clock every afternoon Dan donned huge leg guards and gauntleted gloves, grasped his broad stick and stood heroically in front of the cage which Alf had set on the gymnasium floor and did his best to stop the hard rubber disks that the others sent whizzing or hurtling at him. He got many hard knocks at first, for a puck can make one wince if it manages to come in contact with an unprotected part of one's anatomy, and Dan had his moments of discouragement. But Alf kept him at it.

"You're doing finely," he declared. "And when we get out on the ice you'll like it better."

But they were not destined to get out on the ice just then, for there wasn't any ice. December had apparently made up its mind to be an imitation November. It snowed now and then, and the mornings and evenings were nippy, and there were plenty of cloudy, disagreeable days, but really cold weather avoided the vicinity of Wissining until Christmas vacation arrived. Meanwhile the only event to disturb the even tenor of existence at Yardley was the Winter Debate between Oxford and Cambridge Societies. This came two days before the end of the term and for a week ahead excitement ran high. Every fellow displayed either the light blue of Cambridge or the dark blue of Oxford and enthusiasm bubbled over. No one that we know very well took part for either side. Nor do I remember now the subject for debate. But I do know that it was very weighty, and that Cambridge had the negative side, and that the judges, Messrs. Fry, Austin and Gaddis, of the faculty, remained out quite awhile before rendering their verdict. Tom said this was to avoid having to listen to the efforts of the Glee and Banjo Clubs, but Tom was insufferable that evening, anyhow. He sat with Dan and Alf and Gerald and applauded Oxford's speakers vehemently and groaned whenever a Cambridge man opened his mouth. He pretended that there was no possibility of doubt as to the result.

"It's all Oxford," he declared smugly. "We beat you on logic and eloquence. We have proved conclusively that—that—well, whatever it was is so. You haven't a leg to stand on. The affirmative wins all along the line."

"You wait until you hear from the jury," said Alf darkly. "You fellows had the poorest lot of debaters that ever driveled. Why, that second speaker of yours didn't know the subject! Just worked a lot of musty jokes, and——"

But at that moment the judges returned to the hall, the Glee Club cut off the last verse of the song they were struggling with and Mr. Austin advanced smilingly to the front of the platform.

"Good old Stevie," murmured Tom. "He knows!"

"Yes, and you'll know in a minute," whispered Dan.

That wasn't literally correct, for Mr. Austin had several things to say before he announced the verdict. In Alf's language, he walked around the stump a dozen times. He said nice things about Cambridge and nice things about Oxford. He complimented each speaker and indulged in a few criticisms. And finally he awarded the victory to Oxford!

Wearers of the dark blue arose and made Rome howl. Tom also arose, pulling down his vest and assuming the air of virtue triumphant, but he sat down again very forcibly, and Dan and Alf vented their disappointment on him until he was glad to subside from the settee and beg mercy from the floor. As they were in the back of the hall, and as nothing they might have done could have been heard above the noise, they made Tom perjure himself over and over; made him declare that Cambridge had won the debate fairly, without a shadow of a doubt, that the judges were biased, ignorant and mendacious, that he personally didn't know oratory from a ham sandwich, and that Cambridge was the greatest debating society the world had ever known. Then, after he had cheered for Cambridge — twice, because the first time he had spoiled the effect by giggling — they allowed him to get up. Somehow in the operation of arising he managed to upset the bench backward, and in the subsequent confusion they departed hurriedly from the hall.

Two days later school was depopulated of all save a few boys who lived too far away to travel home for vacation and who had not been invited to spend the ten days with friends. Gerald, Tom, Alf and Dan traveled together as far as New York. Gerald remained there, while Tom crossed to his home in New Jersey and Dan accompanied Alf to Philadelphia. Dan's own home was in Ohio, and as the trip there and back would have spoiled four of the precious days of vacation, he had gladly accepted Alf's invitation to visit him.

CHAPTER XIX
THE HOCKEY TEAM AT WORK

A gray day, still and cold. The river winding away into the misty distance, a green ribbon of glaring ice. A thin powder of crisp snow over the frozen earth and a feeling in the air as of more to come. From the buildings on the hill the smoke rises straight up, blue-gray against the neutral tint of the sky. From the rink by the river comes the sound of voices ringing sharply on the motionless air and the metallic clanging and scraping of skates on the hard ice. The Yardley Hockey Team is at practice. School has been open a week and, although St. John's has fallen victim to the prowess of the blue-stockinged skaters by the score of two goals to none, Alf is far from satisfied with the work of his charges and to-day that much abused word "strenuous" best describes what is going on.

Alf has got his boards and an eight-inch barrier surrounds the rink, the planks being nailed to stakes driven into the ground and their lower edges frozen solid in the margin of the ice. Beyond the boards is a retaining wall of earth some eighteen inches high from the top of which at the present moment some twenty or thirty spectators, well wrapped against the cold, are watching practice. Two benches, borrowed from the tennis courts, are piled with sweaters and extra paraphernalia.

At this end of the rink, his knees bent behind the big padded leg guards and his body unconsciously following, with his eyes, every move of the puck, stands Dan, one hand resting on the top of the goal and the other grasping his broad stick. In front of him Alf is poised at point. Then comes Felder at cover point. The forwards just at present are inextricably mixed with the Second Team players, but three of them you know by sight at least; Goodyear and Roeder playing the centers of the line and Durfee at right end. The left end is Hanley, a Second Class boy.

The Second Team consists to-day of Norcross at goal, Sommers at point, Coke at cover point, and Dick French, Arthur Thompson, Dickenson, and Longwell as forwards. Along the barrier are the substitutes of both teams, three of whom we know; Gerald

Pennimore and Eisner and Ridge of the football eleven. Dickenson is captain and under his leadership the Second is putting up a strong game these days. Along the side of the rink, following the play, skates Andy Ryan, his twinkling green eyes ever watching for offside play and his whistle ever ready to signal a cessation of hostilities. It does so now, and the players pause and lean panting on their sticks while Andy captures the puck. Dickenson and Roeder face-off, the puck is dropped and play begins again. Dickenson captures the puck, and the Second's line is quickly formed to sweep down the rink. Dickenson passes clear across to French. Hanley checks him for an instant, but he recovers the disk and slides it across to Arthur. Then the First Team's defense takes a hand. Felder hurls himself at Arthur, but the puck slips aside just in the nick of time, and Dickenson, whirling about a half-dozen yards from goal, eludes Hanley and shoots. Alf has been put out of the play by Longwell and the puck skims by him knee-high, and in spite of Dan's efforts with stick and body lodges cosily in a corner of the net. The attack waves its sticks wearily and turns back up the ice as Andy blows his whistle. The score is three to two now in favor of the First, and there remains but a few minutes of the second half. Gerald, who has been appointed timekeeper, announces the fact from the side. So both teams put in their substitutes, and Gerald, eagerly handing the stop-watch over to Goodyear, pulls his ulster off and leaps the boards. Besides Goodyear, Felder, Durfee, and Roeder retire from the First. Sanderson takes Felder's place, and Eisner, Gerald, and Ridge play forward.

The puck goes back to the center of the ice, Dickenson and Ridge face-off, the whistle blows and the struggle begins again. Back comes the rubber to Goodyear and down the rink sweep the First's line, low and hard, the puck traveling back and forth across the powdered surface. Down goes Ridge with a crash and a splintered stick, but the remaining three are still line-abreast. Then the Second's cover point flies out, there is a wild mêlée in front of goal, and away skims the puck. Gerald reaches it, but is quickly shouldered across the barrier, and Dickenson steals away toward the First's goal, the disk sliding along easily at the point of his stick. Eisner flies to challenge him, Dickenson passes too late, and once more the First is sweeping toward the enemy's goal. Hanley passes to Ridge ten yards from the net and Ridge, eluding the opposing point, carries the puck on, with Eisner close behind him. Sticks clash and skates grind; Eisner goes down carrying Sommers with him; the puck flies here and there in front of goal; and then Gerald, slipping in between the battling players, reaches the rubber with the tip of his stick and, before he is swept aside, slides it past the goal-tender's foot. Andy's whistle announces a score and stops play.

"Good work, Gerald!" cries Alf from down the rink.

"Time's up!" announces Goodyear.

"Let's have another five minutes, Andy," Dickenson begs. But Andy shakes his head.

"You've had enough. You're tired. That's all to-day."

The spectators hurry away up the hill in the gathering twilight, and the players, after removing their skates and donning coats and sweaters, follow by ones and twos and threes, discussing the play, explaining and arguing. The talk lasts all through the subsequent half hour in the gymnasium while the shower baths are hissing, while bruises are being examined by the watchful trainer and while the boys are getting into their clothes again. By this time appetites are at top-notch, and anyone who has ever played two fifteen-minute halves of a hockey game after a half-hour's practice on a cold afternoon will know why.

The first number of the *Scholiast* issued after the beginning of the new term contained a schedule of the Hockey's Team's contests, and all agreed that French had done his work well. St. John's was followed by Greenburg High School on the 13th. Then came Carrel's School on the 17th, Warren Hall on the 23d, and the Yale Freshmen on the 30th. Nordham came on February 6th, Rock Hill College on the 13th, and the season ended with the Broadwood game on the 20th.

They talked it over that night in 7 Dudley, Alf and Tom and Dan. It was a cold, windy night, the steam pipes were chugging and there was a glowing coal fire in the grate. The three boys had pulled their chairs close to the hearth and were toasting their knees comfortably. Examinations had begun, and it had been a hard day for all of them, but they had each weathered the perils and now were enjoying their reward.

"Did you read this?" asked Tom, holding up his copy of the *Scholiast*.

"Joe's editorial?" asked Dan lazily. "Yes. Great, isn't it?"

"It ought to make a big hit with faculty," said Alf. "I love that about 'a realization of our duty toward those who have patiently and tirelessly sought to instill into our minds the knowledge which in after years—in after years—' I've forgotten the rest. But it's perfectly scrumptious!"

"Oh, Joe's a wonder when he rumples his hair and looks wild-eyed," said Tom. "He will make Horace Greeley and the rest of our great journalists look like base imitations when he gets started. Did you see the hockey schedule, Alf?"

"Yes, and for a wonder they got it right. It's a pretty good schedule, Dan."

"Yes, but when I think of how many bruises I got in the St. John's game and then multiply them by the number of games to come my courage fails. I guess I'll be a fit candidate for the infirmary about the middle of the season."

"Oh," laughed Alf, "you'll soon learn to get the puck with your hand instead of your body. It's a great mistake to try and stop it with your head, Dan."

Dan felt of a lump just over his forehead.

"I guess you're right; especially since if I had got out of the way of that one it would have gone out of the rink, whereas by stopping it with my head it fell in front of goal, and some malicious idiot knocked it in before I had stopped studying astronomy!"

"Accidents will happen," remarked Tom sagely.

"You bet they will! And I'm going to take out an accident policy. I'm beginning to look like a tattooed man, I'm so full of nice little black and blue and yellow spots! I can tell you one thing, Alfred Loring, and that is that if I had known that playing goal was the next thing to being trampled underfoot by an automobile or a trolley car you could have looked somewhere else for a victim!"

"I should think he would want to play the position himself," said Tom. "It's the most responsible position on the team and I think a captain ought to occupy it, don't you, Dan?"

"I wish he would for a while," answered Dan, with enthusiasm. "As it is, I stand there with my eyes popping out of my head while what seem to be about fifty fellows come charging down on me with the puck doing a shuttle act in front of them. I try to watch the puck and the players at the same time and resolve to sell my life dearly. Then, just when they are on me, Alf here dashes gloriously into the fray, always trying to check the man who hasn't had the puck for five minutes. They just open up and let him through—or they put out a stick and he does a double tumble—and they proceed to try and kill the goal-tend."

"And usually succeed," said Tom with a grin. "I've played goal myself."

"Yes, they usually have plenty of fun with me, whether they get the puck in or not. I try to make myself big enough to cover the whole opening, but I can't do it. So I dodge around from this side to that and do a sort of war dance on my skates and flourish my stick about. And all that time they're rapping me on the hands and banging my ankles, and the puck looks like twenty pucks and is all over the shop. And usually Alf is lying on his back on the ice yelling, 'Get it away from there! Get it away from there!'"

Alf joined in the laugh. "Well, Dan," he said, "you see I play point, and the point is to keep out of danger."

"That's a sorry jest," groaned Tom.

"It's worse than that," said Dan. "How's basket ball getting on, by the way?"

"Fine and dandy," Tom answered. "We do up Broadwood a week from Saturday; first game, you know."

"Here or at Broadwood?"

"Here. And, say, you chaps, can't you come along to New York with us on the thirtieth? It's our first trip to the metropolis and we're feeling sort of stuck up about it. Collins wouldn't think of it at first, but I showed him that we could leave here in the morning and get back for supper; so he consented."

"I'm afraid we can't, Tom," said Alf, "for we have an engagement right here that afternoon. The Yale Freshmen play us, you know."

"That's so; I'd forgotten. Well, you can howl for us when we play Broadwood. We've got a pretty good team this year, Alf. That chap, Short, is the best center we've ever had."

"Short? He's the fellow played substitute last year, isn't he?" Alf asked. "A little sawed-off about six feet high?"

"That's the man," laughed Tom. "There's nothing short about him except his name. He doesn't really have to throw the ball into the basket; he just reaches up and drops it in!"

There was a knock on the door, and in response to the dual shout of "Enter, thou!" from Alf and Tom, Gerald appeared.

"Greetings, Mr. Pennimore!" cried Alf. "Kindly close the door behind you and remove your wraps."

Gerald had no wraps to remove, however, and Dan got after him. "You ought to know better than to run around without even a sweater, Gerald. You'll catch cold and have pneumonia or something the first thing you know."

"But I wasn't cold, really," protested Gerald, blowing on his fingers as he took the chair Alf had pulled to the fire.

"That's nonsense," returned Dan sternly. "It isn't smart to do things like this, Gerald. It's just taking risks."

Alf winked gravely at Tom.

"I'm glad I haven't any children," he murmured. "Well, Gerald, how do you like hockey?"

"Very much, only—I don't get much chance to play, Alf."

"Didn't you get in for a while this afternoon, kid?"

"Yes, just for about three or four minutes."

"Well, you must remember that there are quite a few fellows who have played longer than you have, Gerald. Besides, if you will pardon personalities, you are just a little bit light."

"Yes, I know," agreed Gerald mournfully. "If I was only about twenty pounds heavier I'd be all right." He looked wonderingly at the others as they laughed.

"You're all right as you are," answered Alf heartily. "We'll make a hockey player of you yet. But I don't honestly think, Gerald, that you need expect to make the First much before next year."

Gerald's face fell, and his disappointment was so evident that Tom tried to break the force of the blow.

"Anyway, Gerald, you've had pretty near enough glory for one year, haven't you? Making the Cross-Country Team and winning the meet with Broadwood was going some for a youngster."

"But they don't give you your Y for that," said Gerald.

"Oh, so that's it?" said Alf. "Well, you mustn't think about such things, kid. You must always play for the School with no thought of reward." He looked gravely at Tom. Tom grinned.

"Didn't you think about getting your Y when you began to play football?" asked Gerald suspiciously. Alf cleared his throat, and Tom and Dan laughed.

"We-ll, now you're getting personal," he replied evasively. "I won't say the thought didn't occur to me—for a moment—now and then, Gerald, but—er—theoretically——"

"Oh, forget it," said Tom. "Don't talk nonsense. Half the fun is in winning your letter. I was as proud as a peacock when I got mine. They gave them out one afternoon and the next morning I was wearing it on my cap."

"How did you get it?" asked Gerald eagerly.

"Throwing the hammer."

"Do you think I could do that, Tom?"

"I'm afraid not," laughed the other. "But I tell you what you might do, Gerald. You might come out with the track team in the spring and try running the mile. I wouldn't be surprised if you could do that distance pretty well. You've got a mighty nice stride, son."

"I'd like to try it," said Gerald thoughtfully. "I believe I could run the mile rather well."

"Gerald, you are certainly getting a good opinion of yourself," said Dan dryly. "Have you considered pitching for the nine this year?"

"No, but I'll bet I could learn to pitch," answered Gerald untroubledly. "I know how to throw the out drop and the in drop now."

"You might mention that to Durfee," said Dan. "Meanwhile I'm going to my downy." He arose and limped exaggeratedly toward the door. "Say, Alf, does the hockey management supply liniment? If it does I'd like to make arrangements for about six gallons to take me through the season. Come on, Gerald. If you think you'll be too warm going back you might take your coat over your arm."

"Dan, you're peevish to-night," said Alf. "You'll feel better to-morrow after you've stopped a few hot ones with your head."

"And after I've taken two more exams. How did you get on to-day, Gerald?"

"All right, I think," replied Gerald cheerfully. "When does the track team begin work, Tom?"

"Never you mind about track work," said Dan, hustling him out by the nape of his neck. "You come home and do some studying. Good night, fellows."

"Good night, Mr. Grouch!"

At the outer door Dan turned to Gerald: "Now you run like the dickens all the way across. If you don't I'll rub your face with snow. And another time if I catch you parading around in this weather with nothing on——"

But Gerald was already racing across the yard for Clarke.

CHAPTER XX
FIRST BLOOD FOR YARDLEY

January dragged past and examinations came to an end with no serious results for any of these in whom we are interested. The hockey team defeated Greenburg easily, lost to Carrel's school, 3 to 7, won from Warren Hall, 18 to 2, and finished the month with a well-played game in which the Yale Freshmen took its measure to the tune of 12 to 4. All the month the ice remained in perfect condition, although the team was kept pretty busy shoveling snow from the rink. Dan had settled down into his game at goal and, while he still pretended that Alf had persuaded him to join the team in the hope of having him killed, he enjoyed it all hugely and was fast developing into a strong and steady player. Gerald still adorned the edge of the ice most of the time, although in the Warren game he played part of one half and, being opposed to fellows not much heavier than he, played rather well and had two goals to his credit.

Basket ball had its devotees and regularly twice a week Yardley met an opponent. So far Tom's team had been defeated but twice and had played seven games. The first Broadwood game had resulted in a tie at 17 to 17, although three extra periods had been played. Yardley had won the second contest at Broadwood by a decisive score, 22 to 12, and the third meeting, which it was hoped would decide the championship, was due in a week. Gerald was the only one of our friends who accompanied the basket ball team to New York on the thirtieth. It had been his custom since Thanksgiving to spend Sunday in the city with his father, and as there was no hope of his getting into the hockey game with the Yale Freshmen that afternoon, he elected to accompany Tom and the team to New York. The team met defeat after a hard battle and from the up-town gymnasium, in which the contest had taken place, Gerald walked down to his home, only a few blocks distant. When he returned to school early Monday morning February had arrived with mild weather. The next day, under the influence of a south wind and warm sunlight, the ice on the rink began to soften and rot, and, although the team managed to hold practice that afternoon, it proved to be the last for over a week. The Nordham game, set for the sixth, had to be cancelled and Alf went around like a bear with a sore head.

It was about this time that the Pennimore Cup arrived. Alf and Dan and Gerald walked down to the express office one noon and bore it back in triumph. They opened the box in Dan's room, and after sprinkling the floor with excelsior, drew the cup from its flannel bag and viewed it with delight. It was of silver, some ten inches in height and most elaborately designed. On one side, in relief, were three figures of hockey players scrimmaging for the puck. On the other side was the raised inscription "Pennimore Cup for Hockey—Won By," and below it a shield for recording the winners' names. There were two curving handles in the form of hockey sticks and flag poles from which the rival banners of Yardley and Broadwood swept away around the rim of the cup. The inside was gilded and there was an ebony base to set it on. They placed it on the table and gazed at it enrapturedly.

"It's the handsomest cup I ever saw!" said Dan.

"It's a—a peach!" said Alf. "Gerald, your dad was certainly good to us."

"I wish he could see it," murmured Gerald.

"He will, for it's going to stay right here at Yardley," declared Alf. "We've just *got* to win that, Dan!"

"You bet we have!"

"You look after it to-night and to-morrow we'll take it over to Greenburg and get Proctor to exhibit it in his window for a week or so; that will give the Broadwood fellows a chance to see it."

"I hope they'll never get a better chance," said Dan.

News of the trophy's arrival was soon about school and during the evening there was a steady stream of visitors invading No. 28, and the following day Alf and Gerald and Dan took the cup to Greenburg and arranged with the amiable Mr. Proctor to place it in his window. Mr. Proctor conducted the principal book and stationery store and held the trade of both schools. Alf wrote an explanatory card to be placed with the cup: "Pennimore Cup, the gift of Mr. John T. Pennimore, to be contested for at hockey by Broadwood and Yardley, and to become the permanent possession of the school winning two out of three games." Then they went out on the sidewalk and blocked traffic while they had a good look at it.

"Bet you that will make Broadwood's eyes stick out," said Alf. "Let's wait here awhile until some Broadwoods come along and hear what they say."

"Don't you suppose they'd know who you are, you silly chump?" laughed Dan. "Come on home."

"Not until I've had a hot chocolate," returned Alf firmly, moving away from the window with a lingering look at the silver cup. "Want one? My treat."

"In that case we'll each take two," answered Dan.

"I'll have an egg-and-chocolate," said Gerald.

"Why?" asked Dan innocently. "Is it more?"

"You dry up or you won't get anything," said Alf as he ushered them through the door of the drug store. "Two hot chocolates and an egg-and-chocolate, please," he announced to the clerk at the fountain.

"Hold on a bit," interrupted Dan soberly. "I haven't decided what mine is." He looked about at the signs dangling in front of him. "'Walnut Fudge Sundæ'; what do you suppose that is, Alf?"

"I don't know, but it's too cold for ice-cream things."

"That's so. Let me see, then. 'Hot Malted Milk'; that won't do; I had to take that once when I had a cold and the doctor wouldn't let me eat real food."

"Oh, hurry up, can't you?" begged Alf. "Have a hot choc——"

"Ah! There it is, I'll bet! 'Hot Celery Wine'; sounds wicked, doesn't it? Hot Celery Wine's the drink for mine; it's strong and fine and makes you shine——"

"Give it to him!" Alf exploded. "Give him a fried egg with it and let him have a real party!"

"No, no, I guess Hot Celery Wine would be too strong. I'll have a hot chocolate."

The clerk, visibly amused, served the order and added a little dish of sweet crackers, and the boys removed their repast to one of the small tables near by from where they could view the street through the big window.

"There are some Broadwoods now," said Alf, "looking at the cup. I'd like to hear what they're saying." Dan leaned past him so that he could see Proctor's window.

"The big fellow is Rhodes, their full back," he said. "Here come a couple of them over here."

The two Broadwood fellows entered, ordered raspberry college ices, and sat down at a table a few feet distant. They had recognized Alf at once and possibly Dan, but they strove to hide the fact.

"What did you think of it?" asked one.

"Oh, not so bad," was the reply. "Of course it isn't really silver; you can see that quick enough."

"Of course," replied the other scornfully. "Probably tin, don't you think?"

"Or pewter. They're using pewter a good deal for cups."

"Ugly shape, isn't it? I suppose, though, that Yardley thinks it's quite wonderful. I guess they don't see many cups over there."

They laughed softly and bent over their ices in order to exchange glances. Gerald was angry clean through and Alf was scowling into the bottom of his glass.

"Who's this fellow Pennimore?" asked one of the Broadwood lads.

"He's a rich guy that lives over on the point. He's got a son at Yardley. The kid tried to get into Broadwood but couldn't pass, and they say the old man promised to pay off the school debt at Yardley if they'd take the kid. Anyhow, he's there."

Gerald set his glass down and started to his feet with blazing cheeks, but Dan's hand went out and caught his arm.

"No, you don't," said Dan firmly. "You sit down again."

"But— —"

"You sit down!" Gerald obeyed. Alf had stopped frowning. He finished his chocolate, wiped his lips with the little paper napkin and leaned across smilingly to Dan.

"You and Gerald walk to the door," he said softly, "and be ready to get away quick."

"What are you going to do?" asked Dan.

"Well, I'm not going to touch them, if that's what you mean," answered Alf. "Go ahead and I'll follow."

Dan and Gerald arose and sauntered toward the door, the Broadwood boys observing them uneasily, although defiantly. Alf took up the three empty glasses and started toward the counter. To reach it he had to pass the table occupied by the Broadwood fellows, and as he did so he stumbled, fell against the table and sent the college ices to the tiled floor where the cups broke and their contents splashed about for yards. One of the boys saved the table from going over and both jumped angrily to their feet.

"What do you mean by that?"

"Sorry," answered Alf indifferently, "but you ought to keep your feet out of the way."

"Our feet weren't in your way! You did it on purpose!"

"How absurd," said Alf haughtily, as the clerk hurried up with towels. "As though I would intentionally upset the table. I have more respect for cups than you have."

He sauntered over to the counter, set his glasses down and joined Dan and Gerald at the door. The Broadwood boys were excitedly explaining to the proprietor who had followed his clerk to the scene. Dan and Gerald and Alf slipped quietly out of the door, trying hard to keep sober countenances. But once out of sight of the window they hugged each other ecstatically and laughed to their heart's content.

"They'll have to pay for damages," gurgled Alf, "and I'll bet they haven't got fifty cents between them!"

"Maybe Wallace will get after us for it," said Dan.

"Oh, no, he won't. He isn't taking any chances. He's got those chaps and he knows he may not see us again. Besides, he wouldn't suspect for a moment that I'd do a thing like that on purpose! Perish the thought! First bloodshed in the conflict for the Pennimore Cup results in a Yardley victory! Ex-tra! Ex-tra!"

CHAPTER XXI
THE BASKET BALL GAME

Dan opened the window and thrust his head out.

"The enemy approaches," he announced. Below him, up the hill, approached the Broadwood barge, its lamps boring holes in the darkness. He could hear the straining of the horses, the crunch of wheels on the gravel and the voices of the occupants. "What time is it?" he asked, closing the window again with a shiver.

"Twenty-five to eight," replied Gerald, laying his book down with an expression of relief. "Let's go over."

"It's a bit early. We'll walk over and get Alf first. Put your coat on, chum. It's as cold as they make it to-night."

A quarter of an hour later the three of them were sitting in the front row of the balcony at the gymnasium doing their share of the cheering which had burst forth as the Yardley Basket Ball Team had trotted onto the floor. Broadwood appeared a moment later and for ten minutes the baskets quivered under the assaults of the balls as the players danced back and forth and shot at goal. The cheering kept up, for everyone was in high spirits at the prospect of a decisive victory over Broadwood in the final contest. Broadwood had sent a dozen or two supporters who had congregated at one corner of the floor and were heroically encouraging their team. At a few minutes past eight the referee, athletic director of the Greenburg Y. M. C. A., called the teams together. Goals were chosen and the Blue and the Green arranged themselves about the floor. Up went the ball in the ring and Short, stretching his long arm high in air, tipped it back to Tom. A pass across the floor, a second pass to a waiting guard, a step forward and an easy toss and the ball dropped through Yardley's basket for the first score in something under two seconds. Yardley cheered and stamped and a black 2 appeared on the board opposite the Y.

Two more easy baskets followed before Broadwood pulled herself together. Then her defense covered closer and, although Yardley pushed the war into the enemy's territory time and again during the succeeding ten minutes, she was unable to add to the 6 she had secured. Short's ability at center handicapped Broadwood, for that tall youth was able, nine times out of ten, to put the ball in any direction he pleased. Usually it went to Tom, who played right forward, and who was so quick and certain at passing that the ball was under Yardley's goal before the defense was aware of it. But after the first ten minutes of play Broadwood's captain worked an improvement in the work of his team. They covered better and Tom found that his opponent had taken on the semblance of a leech and was always at his elbow, no matter how hard he tried to shake him off. Broadwood made her first score from a free try after a Yardley player had been detected holding and the little knot of Blue adherents in the corner cheered lustily. That 1 on the board seemed to bring encouragement and the Green set to work furiously. A long and lucky shot from almost the middle of the floor brought cries of approval from even the Yardley throng and made the score 6 to 3.

The play was roughing up a good deal and presently a double foul was called. Yardley failed at her attempt and Broadwood succeeded, and again the score changed.

"Come on, now!" called Tom. "Stop that fouling and get busy!"

In response Yardley worked through the Broadwood defense by pretty team work and scored again, but that was the last basket of the period and the twenty minutes ended with the figures on the board 8 to 4 in favor of the home team.

During the ten minutes intermission Yardley amused herself singing songs, while from the floor at intervals came faintly the sound of Broadwood's cheers.

"Well, that's a good margin to begin the next half on," said Alf contentedly. "But it doesn't look to me that Tom's aggregation of world beaters is quite up to form. What do you think, Dan?"

"They're slow. Tom's been driving them all the way. We haven't got this old game yet, Alf."

"Oh, we'll have it all right. Here they come."

Broadwood had made two changes in her team and the changes worked for the better. The new men were lighter in weight but far speedier, and, moreover, they were fresh and untired. From the start of the last half the Blue began to overhaul her rival. The 4 changed to a 6, and then to an 8, and the score was tied. Over the edge of the balcony hung a fringe of shouting, gesticulating red-faced youths. A foul was called on Broadwood and Yardley led by one point. Then followed a long and desperate throw by a Yardley forward which in some miraculous way got through the basket.

"That's the stuff, fellows!" shouted Tom, racing back to his position and fighting off his too-affectionate opponent. "We've got them on the run now! Play it up!"

For once Short missed the toss and the ball sped away toward a Broadwood forward. The center raced down the floor as the ball came back to him. A Yardley guard dived toward him, the center feinted and let him go sprawling by. Short engaged him from behind and for a moment gave him all he could do. Then a Blue youth eluded his man, took the ball at a short pass and threw it backwards and over his head for one of the prettiest goals of the evening.

For some reason that appeared to demoralize Yardley. She fought desperately and wildly, but her men forgot team play and it was everyone for himself. Tom begged and commanded, but dissolution had the team. Twice Broadwood scored from the floor because the Yardley defense, over-anxious, had allowed itself to be coaxed away from goal, and twice she won points from free tries. If she had thrown all the baskets Yardley's penalties allowed she would have had several more figures to her credit. Toward the end of the period Tom, hopeless of bringing back order to his team, took things into his own hands in a desperate effort to retrieve the day. Twice he scored almost unaided and the shouts from the balcony crashed against the walls. But Broadwood, aware now of her superiority, played together like well-drilled soldiers and score after score followed. During the last five minutes it was a veritable rout and when the bell clanged the score was Yardley, 15, Broadwood, 27, and down on the floor a group of delighted youths were doing a dance and trying hard to cheer a hole through the roof.

Dan and Alf and Gerald waited for Tom and walked back to Dudley with him. Tom was disappointed but philosophical.

"We simply went to pieces," he said. "It was every fellow on his own hook with us in the second half, while Broadwood played together like veterans, which most of them are. If we'd kept up our team play we could have tied them or won. I guess these little things have to happen, though, and, after all, she hasn't beaten us in the series."

"Will you play her again, Tom?" asked Gerald anxiously.

"I'd like to, but faculty won't let us. No, it's a stand-off this year. We'll get back at them next year, though. They're pretty sure to make Short captain, and he's a good player and has a head on his shoulders."

"Well, we mustn't expect to win all down the line," said Dan comfortingly. "We beat at football and cross-country and we have a good show at baseball."

"Not to speak of hockey," added Alf.

"What's the matter with the track meet?" inquired Tom. "I'll bet we'll simply freeze her out this spring. Why, we've got all the sprints and most of the field events cinched."

"And Gerald is going to run in the mile," said Alf. "So you can add that, too."

"I really am going to try," said Gerald earnestly. "Tom says I can make the team, even if I don't win points."

"Why not?" asked Alf, with a wink at Dan. "That's an easy way to get your Y. Look at Tom. He'd never have got it any other way!"

"He's got it in three things," said Gerald enviously.

"Oh, that's just because when you once win it nobody cares how many more you get," said Alf carelessly. "It's like shinning up a tree. After you get to the first branch the rest is easy."

"I—I wish I could get to the first branch then," laughed Gerald.

"Oh, you will. Just keep on shinning."

That day the warm spell had disappeared, and when Dan and Gerald returned to Clarke there was a bitter northwest wind blowing.

"This means plenty of ice to-morrow," said Dan.

The ice was there, but it was in such rough shape that it was necessary to re-flood the rink sufficiently to get a new surface, and instead of hockey practice on Monday afternoon the team had manual labor. Unfortunately Mr. McCarthy's pump had given out, and so, after some study of the problem, Alf organized a bucket brigade. It was cold work dipping water from a hole in the river ice and carrying it by pailfuls a good thirty yards to the nearer corner of the rink. The water froze around the rim of the buckets and the ice had to be knocked away after every third or fourth trip. And it was hard on hands, too. But there were twenty odd boys in the brigade, each with a bucket, and at last the old surface was flooded over. That was on Monday, and on the following Saturday was to come the last game before the Broadwood contest and Alf was impatient to get back to practice. The enforced idleness showed its effect the next afternoon. Muscles were stiff, ankles weak and the fellows went at their work in a slow and half-hearted way that aroused the captain's ire.

"If you fellows don't want to play," he declared sarcastically, "just say so and I'll let you off. But if you do, for goodness sake stop falling over your sticks! Goodyear, you and Roeder had better lay off awhile. Ridge and Pennimore! Come and see if you can at least stay on your feet. Hurry up, now. Let's get some snap into this. You're letting the Second put it all over you."

But the next day the players showed some of their old form and the Second had all it could do to make its single tally. The weather remained cold and the ice hard and firm. On Friday there came indications of a thaw, and it wasn't until after nine o'clock that French was certain enough of the morrow's conditions to go to the telephone and communicate with the manager of the Rock Hill College team. "The ice may be a little soft in spots," he said over the wire, "but there's no doubt but that we can play. So we'll expect you down on the train that gets here at two sixteen. We'll play as soon after that as you're ready." Alf's last act that night before getting into bed was to open the window and put his head out.

"What's it doing?" asked Tom sleepily.

"Sort of cloudy, but it's stopped dripping. It'll probably freeze a little before morning. I wonder who invented the New England climate, anyway. You never know one minute what it's going to do the next."

"I didn't," murmured Tom, turning over in bed with a grunt.

CHAPTER XXII
GERALD GOES ON AN ERRAND

By eleven o'clock the next forenoon the thaw had begun in earnest, but it was too late to cancel the game. Rock Hill appeared on the scene promptly and at a quarter to three the game began. The ice was soft along the boards and there was a film of water everywhere, but it was possible to play for all of that. Felder was out of the game with tonsilitis and Sanderson took his place at cover point. The whole school turned out to see the contest and lined the rink two and three deep. Alf expected a hard game but defeat was not reckoned on. Yet at the end of the first twenty-minute period, with the score 2 to 0 in Rock Hill's favor, it didn't look so improbable. Rock Hill presented a team of older and more experienced players and far excelled Yardley in skating ability and stick work. Had it not been for Dan's really brilliant performance at the cage the score would have been much larger. In the second half Yardley had what benefit there was from the wind, but, in spite of that, the play remained about her goal most of the time and that Rock Hill was able to add but one tally to her score was due to good work on the part of the defense, and the fact that Rock Hill's shooting was not as brilliant as her other game. With the score, 3 to 0, and some four minutes to play, Alf saved the home team from a shut-out by taking the puck himself the length of the rink and, with one short pass to Hanley and back in front of goal, scoring Yardley's only tally. But there was no disgrace in being beaten by Rock Hill, and, on the whole, Yardley's work showed a distinct advance over that of the game with the Yale freshmen. If the Blue could play as well a week from that day, when she was due to meet the Green, Alf believed that the Pennimore Cup and the season's championship would remain at Yardley.

But the weather was to be reckoned with, it seemed, for all Saturday and Sunday and Monday the warm spell continued, until the hockey rink was a shallow puddle of water with not a vestige of ice to be seen. The river broke up and the last of the snow melted in the drifts. The weather was almost springlike and Alf fumed and fretted and studied the predictions. And, meanwhile, the only practice to be obtained was in the gymnasium where, with two Indian clubs set up to indicate a goal, the fellows shot until their arms ached.

But winter was only sulking in his tent, and on Tuesday morning the thermometer began to go down. By night the mercury was hovering about thirty and Alf went to sleep hopefully. The ground was hard in the morning, but the noon sun thawed it out again. Alf never entered or emerged from Oxford that he didn't pause to scowl at the big thermometer by the door. Toward evening a breeze sprang out of the north and the mercury dropped ten degrees in half an hour. Moreover, it continued to drop all night and in the morning it showed twenty-one degrees. The weather was cloudy and at noon it was snowing fitfully. The rink was frozen smooth and hard and practice began again that afternoon. Alf once more wore a cheerful countenance. In the locker room at the gymnasium afterwards he called across to Gerald: "Say, Gerald, we've got to get that cup back before the game. Do you mind doing it? You'd better run over tomorrow if you can find time."

"All right," answered Gerald. "I'll attend to it, Alf. I suppose he will give it to me, won't he?"

"Who? Proctor? I guess so, but I'll give you an order. Remind me to write it this evening."

Gerald's opportunity came after dinner the following day. He had no recitations between two and three and so, armed with Alf's note to the store proprietor, he tramped over to Greenburg in the teeth of a northeast gale and got the cup. He wanted very much to warm himself with a hot chocolate, but they had agreed that it would be wise to stay away from Wallace's until last week's episode of the broken glasses had been forgotten, and, since Wallace's was the only place where they knew how to prepare a hot chocolate properly, Gerald was forced to start on his homeward trip without refreshment. The cup was in its maroon-colored flannel bag and he tucked it under his arm so that his hands might have the benefit of his coat pockets. When he reached the bridge over the river he heard his name called and, looking down, saw Harry Merrow on the ice. There were several other boys with him, mostly youngsters, and Jake Hiltz was sitting near by struggling with a refractory skate strap.

"Going to skate?" asked Harry. Gerald shook his head and danced up and down in the effort to bring warmth into his numbed toes. Harry eyed the maroon bag.

"What are you doing with your skates, then?" he inquired.

"It's not skates," said Gerald. "It's the hockey cup. I've been over to Greenburg for it."

"Oh, I thought you had your skates there. Why don't you get them and come on down? The ice is dandy."

"I've got hockey practice in half an hour, Harry."

"Oh, I forgot. Are you going to make the team? Arthur says you're a good player."

"I won't make it this year, I guess," Gerald answered. "Isn't it cold? I must go on or I'll freeze fast to the bridge here."

In his room he took the cup out of the bag and set it on the table, tossing the bag aside, and while he warmed himself at the radiator he admired it and wondered whether Yardley would be able to keep it out of the clutches of her rival. It would, he reflected, be an awful shame if Broadwood should succeed in winning it for good. But whoever won it, he was going to see that there was another cup to take its place. After awhile it occurred to him that if he was not going to be late for hockey practice he would have to hurry. So he left the room, ran downstairs and sped across the yard to the gymnasium. Alf and some of the others were just starting down to the rink as he reached the door.

"I got the cup, Alf," he said. "It's in my room. Shall I bring it over this evening?"

"Why, no, you might as well keep it until Saturday, I guess. Get your togs on, Gerald, and hurry down. If Andy comes in tell him I've gone ahead."

There was a stiff practice that afternoon, a good three quarters of an hour of it, followed by two twenty-minute periods with the Second Team, for to-morrow's session was to be brief and light, only sufficient to keep muscles limber. Gerald took part in the preliminary work and then wrapped himself against the cold and

Winning His "Y": A Story of School Athletics

became official timekeeper while the First and Second Teams went at each other hammer and tongs. The weather was conducive to fast work, and in the first period Alf's players managed to score four goals to the Second's one. In the second half all the substitutes had their chances and Gerald tried his best to make good. But he was over-anxious and, being light, always got the worst of it in a mix-up. Eager to distinguish himself, he over-skated time and again and lost the puck, and Alf called constant warnings to him.

"Careful, Gerald! There, you've done it again! Use both hands on that stick, man! You can't do anything that way!"

He turned to Dan and added: "If Gerald could use his stick as well as he can use his skates he would make a good player."

Dan smiled.

"He's probably thinking that this is his last chance this year, Alf, and he wants to make a hit. He— Gee, he will get killed if he tries that sort of thing!"

"Come now, Gerald!" sang out Alf. "This isn't a slugging match! Keep your stick down and look what you're doing. You, too, Roeder! Follow up, man, follow up!"

The Second managed to score twice in that half and the First broke through the opposing defense for four more goals. Then Andy called a halt and, in spite of Alf's pleading for "another five minutes, Andy," drove them off the ice. After they had had their showers and had dressed, Alf and Dan and Gerald left the gymnasium together.

"What was the matter with you this afternoon, Gerald?" asked Alf with a smile. "You looked as though you were trying to kill the whole Second Team."

"Got sort of excited, didn't you, chum?" laughed Dan.

"Well, you mustn't get excited," Alf said. "If you do you can't play good hockey. You've got to keep cool all the time and know just what you're doing. Let the other side lose their heads. If they do you've got the game cinched. Just as soon as you go up in the air you forget all about formation and begin to play the game all by your lonesome. And as soon as you do that you'll find that the other chaps are eating you up, goal after goal. Remember that, kid. Next year you try again. You'll be a good deal heavier then, I guess, and I don't see why you shouldn't make the team. And get your Y," he added with a smile.

"I'm going to get it before then," said Gerald gravely. "I'm going out for the Track Team, you know."

"Of course; I'd forgotten. Well, I hope you win a few points for us, Gerald. For in spite of Tom's blathering I have an idea that it isn't going to be so much of a walk-over after all. You got the cup, you said?"

"Yes. And I wanted a hot chocolate but I didn't dare go into Wallace's for it. I pretty nearly froze coming home."

"Well, if you had gone into Wallace's he might have made it warm for you," laughed Alf. "Coming over this evening, Dan? You'd better. Tom's going to Oxford, I think; they've got one of their amateur vaudeville entertainments on for to-night. Tom just dotes on hearing rag-time music and seeing fellows take paper flowers out of a derby hat."

"Yes, I'll drop in for awhile," answered Dan. "My, but it certainly is cold!"

"It's great! I hope it stays just this way until after Saturday."

"Well, Saturday is bound to be a cold day for somebody," replied Dan. After which *bon mot* he and Gerald scuttled for Clarke.

It was dark when they reached the room, and while Dan found the matches and lighted the gas Gerald took his coat off. He was hanging it on its hook in his closet when Dan spoke.

"Where did you put the cup?" he asked.

"On the table there under your nose," replied Gerald.

"On the table? Well, maybe you did, but it isn't here now."

CHAPTER XXIII
THE CUP DISAPPEARS

"Then you've got it in your hand," said Gerald untroubledly and without turning.

"I haven't! I tell you it isn't here!"

"Not there!" Gerald turned and stared at the table and from the table to Dan's hands and from thence to his face. "But—why, I put it there not two hours ago!"

"Are you sure?" Dan looked about the room. "Didn't you tuck it away in a drawer somewhere?"

"No, I took it out of the bag and put it right here on the table." Gerald placed his hand on the spot. "And then I went over there to the radiator and warmed my hands and feet and looked at it."

"Well, it's mighty funny," grumbled Dan. "You'd better look in your bureau, Gerald."

"But I tell you I left it there, Dan!" Nevertheless Gerald opened the drawers one after the other and peeked in. "It was there when I went out. I didn't touch it after I took it out of the bag."

"What did you do with the bag?" asked Dan, making an unsuccessful search among the cushions of the window seat.

"Tossed it on the table. Isn't it there?"

"Not a sign of it." Dan thrust his hands in his pockets and frowned across at his roommate. "Look here, chum, this is sort of peculiar. Are you certain you went for it?"

"Am I certain—" began Gerald exasperatedly. "Don't be silly, Dan! Of course, I'm certain. I'm not likely to forget it, for I almost froze coming home."

"You didn't drop it on the way? Or leave it anywhere?"

"I brought it up here and put it on the table there," answered Gerald decidedly and a trifle impatiently. "Some one has taken and hidden it; that's all there is to it; and I think it's a pretty poor joke."

"Was anyone with you?"

"No, I was alone. Let's look around the room. Some fellow must have stuck it away somewhere."

"I don't see who could have done that," answered Dan. "I don't believe anyone has been in here this afternoon except you."

"I don't know anything about that," answered Gerald crossly. "I know I left it there and now it's gone. Look under your bed, Dan."

They searched the room thoroughly, looked under the beds and the window seat and the chiffoniers, peered into the dark corners of the closets, pulled things off the shelves, investigated the mattresses and, in short, turned the place upside down. Then they sat down and stared at each other.

"Well, it beats me," said Dan hopelessly. "All I can think is that you imagined it, Gerald."

"I didn't imagine it, I tell you! Did you look thoroughly in your bureau?"

"Yes," Dan replied, but went back to it and took everything out of the drawers, and Gerald did the same with his belongings. Then they lifted photograph frames and looked behind the radiator and searched in equally impossible places. Finally Dan sank into a chair and Gerald subsided on his bed.

"It isn't in this room," said Dan decidedly. "Either you imagined that you brought it up here, Gerald, or some one has been in and taken it away."

"Then some one has taken it," said Gerald decisively. "Do you suppose Tom could have come in and seen it and taken it over to Dudley?"

Dan's face cleared.

"I'll bet that's just what happened," he said. "We'll stop there when we go to supper and find out. It couldn't have been anyone but Tom. Alf was at hockey and no one else would have any right to touch it. Let's wash up and run over there."

"I don't suppose anyone would steal it," said Gerald half questioningly.

"Steal it! Of course not! No one ever gets up here but the fellows and the chambermaids and the faculty. Besides, it isn't likely that a thief would have taken the bag too."

"No, that's so," Gerald agreed. "I guess Tom found it and thought Alf wanted it over there."

But that theory was short-lived. When they reached 7 Dudley they found Tom and Alf just leaving the room to go to commons for supper.

"Say, Tom, did you burglarize our room this afternoon?" asked Dan.

"If I did I'll bet I didn't get much," was the answer. "Why?"

"Didn't you get the cup?"

"The cup? What cup are you talking about?"

"The hockey cup. Quit fooling, Tom. You took it, didn't you?"

Tom saw by the earnest look on Dan's face that that youth was not joking and so he answered seriously:

"I haven't been near your room to-day, Dan. What's up?"

"Why, Gerald says he brought the hockey cup home from Greenburg and put it on the table and left it there when he went to practice. It isn't there now and we've searched high and low for it."

"That's a funny game," said Alf anxiously. "Is that straight, Dan?"

"Yes. The only thing I could think of was that Tom had happened in and taken it over here."

"Have you looked everywhere in the room?"

"Rather! The place looks like a pigsty; we've pulled everything out of the drawers and even looked under the mattresses. Oh, it isn't there, Alf. Some one, I don't know who, has taken it out of that room. I suppose they've done it for a joke, but if I catch them I'll show them who the joke is on."

"Well, let's go over to supper. Afterwards we'll go up to your room and see if we can't find it."

"You're welcome to look," said Dan impatiently, "but I tell you it isn't there."

"Perhaps whoever swiped it will bring it back by that time," said Tom cheerfully. "I guess some fresh chump saw it and thought he'd have some fun with you fellows."

"I'd like to be there when he returned it," growled Dan, as they hurried across to Whitson and supper.

Half an hour later they climbed the stairs to 28. They all more than half expected to see the silver trophy standing on the table when Dan threw the door open. But it wasn't there. Alf made the other three sit down and himself began a systematic search of the premises. At the end of ten minutes, however, he was forced to agree with Dan and Gerald. The Pennimore Cup was not in 28 Dudley, wherever it might be. Dan sat down and took one knee into his hands.

"Now let's get at this thing," he said. "Tell us just what happened after you got to Proctor's store, Gerald."

"I gave him your note and told him I'd come to take the cup back. He went to the window and got it and put it in the flannel bag. I took it and walked home with it and when I got up here——"

"Wait a minute," Alf interrupted. "Didn't you say you stopped and got a hot chocolate somewhere?"

"No, I said I wanted to, but I was afraid that if I went into Wallace's he would recognize me and make a fuss about his broken glasses."

"So you didn't stop anywhere after you left Proctor's?"

"No, not until I got to the bridge."

"The river bridge? Why did you stop there?"

"Because Harry Merrow called to me. He and some other chaps were skating just above the bridge."

"What did he want?" asked Alf.

"He asked if I was going to skate. He thought the bag was a skate bag, you see. I told him I had the cup in it."

"Then what?"

"Then," continued Gerald, trying hard to recall the conversation, "he asked me to go and get my skates and said the ice was fine. I said I had to report for hockey practice. He asked if I expected to make the team and I said not this year. And then I was cold and came on home."

"What did you do with the cup while you were talking?"

"I kept it under my arm."

"Are you sure? You didn't set it down anywhere—say, on the top of the bridge girder?"

"No, it was under my arm all the time."

"All right. You brought it straight up here. Didn't stop anywhere else first?"

"No, I came right up to the room and took the cup out of the bag and put it there. And I tossed the bag about here. Then I went over to the radiator and stood there about ten minutes, I guess, getting my feet and hands warm. And I was looking at the cup and wondering if we would win it. I remember thinking that if Broadwood got it for keeps I'd have dad present another one."

"Good idea, Gerald. Then what happened?"

"Then I remembered that I'd have to hurry to get to practice on time, and so I——"

"Picked up the cup and put it away. Where did you put it?"

"I didn't touch it, Alf! I just left it where it was and went over to the gym."

"Did you close the door as you went out?" asked Tom.

"I—I think so. I'm not sure. I was in a hurry, you know."

"You don't remember hearing it close behind you?"

"N-no, I don't. But I'm sure I *almost* closed it, Tom."

Tom arose and went into the hall, leaving the door some six inches ajar. Then he returned and opened it wider, and finally he came back, closing it behind him.

"The door would have to be almost half open," he reported, "for anyone in the corridor to be able to see the cup where Gerald put it. You're sure you didn't leave it that far open, Gerald?"

"Positive," was the reply. "I may not have latched it, but— —"

"Hold on a minute," Dan interrupted. "The window at the end of the corridor was open at the top this afternoon. I remember that because it was so blamed cold when we came up before supper."

"What do you mean?" asked Alf. "That some one might have got in that window?"

"Of course not! I mean that if there was a draft in the hall this door might have blown open if Gerald didn't latch it as he went out."

"That's so. How was it when you came back?"

"Closed," answered Dan promptly.

"Shut tight," agreed Gerald.

"Looks, then, as though some one might have been in," said Tom.

"Great Scott!" said Dan. "There's no question about that, Tom. Gerald is sure he left the cup here on the table and now it's gone. Some one came in, all right enough, but who was it?"

"Who is this Merrow chap?" asked Tom. "Is he the youngster that rooms with Arthur Thompson, Gerald?"

"Yes," answered Gerald.

"You remember Merrow," said Alf impatiently, "the kid that Gerald and Thompson pulled out of Marsh Lake last spring?"

"Oh, yes. Well, he isn't the sort to try a joke like this, is he? You see, he seems to be the only one that knew Gerald had the cup."

"Not the only one," said Gerald. "There were six or seven other fellows around there; Craig and Milton and—and Bicknell; I don't remember the rest; two or three of them I didn't know. And Hiltz was there, too, only he was farther away."

"Hiltz!" said Dan.

"Hiltz," murmured Alf. The three exchanged questioning glances.

"Was he near enough to hear what you and Merrow were saying?" asked Dan. Gerald considered.

"I don't believe so. He might have heard, though. You know voices sound pretty plain on the ice."

"How far was he from where you were?"

"About seventy-five or eighty feet, I think."

"Was he nearer than that to Merrow?"

"Oh, yes, Merrow was about twenty feet from the bridge. Hiltz was sitting on the bank at the right. I suppose he was fifty feet from Harry."

"What do you think?" asked Alf, turning to Dan. Dan shook his head in a puzzled way.

"I don't know," he said. "He might have. Maybe he thought it would be a good way to get even with the three of us at one fell swoop. By the way, where does he live?"

"In Whitson; second floor," answered Tom. "I don't know his number, though."

"If we could find out what he did after Gerald left him," muttered Dan. "Harry Merrow might know how long he was on the ice."

"Yes, but he might have come in here any time during the two hours from three to five."

"Yes, but if he meant to swipe the cup he would have done it while he was certain that both Gerald and I were at hockey practice, and he would probably have done it early in the afternoon."

"It wouldn't have been a hard thing to do," said Tom. "He knew you were both on the ice, there aren't many fellows around at half past three, say, and on a cold day like this most every fellow that is at home keeps his door closed. He might have walked in here, taken the cup, put it under his coat and walked out again, and no one would have seen him."

"Suppose he did," said Alf. "What do you think he would do with it? Hide it in his room?"

"Not likely, I guess," answered Tom, "but still he might. There are plenty of places around the school he might have put it. If we were only certain he had taken it — —"

"That's the trouble," growled Alf. "We can't go to him and say, 'Hiltz you stole the Pennimore Cup out of Dan's room this afternoon and we want it back!' After all, I don't believe Hiltz is a thief."

"I don't suppose he is," said Dan, "and he probably wouldn't call it thieving. If he has taken it he's done it just to make trouble for us and with no idea of keeping the cup himself. Probably he means to return it before the game, or leave it where it will be found."

"It's just the same as stealing," exclaimed Gerald angrily, "and I'll bet he did it! He knew I had it and he hates me like poison since I beat him in the cross-country, and more since I got into Cambridge. And he hates Dan for defeating him at the election."

"Well, I'm inclined to think you're right, Gerald," said Alf. "But the question before the meeting is: What are we going to do? We've got to get hold of that cup before the game on Saturday, and to-morrow's Friday. We'd look like a pretty lot of idiots if we had to tell Broadwood that we'd lost the cup! I wish we hadn't gone and exhibited it in Proctor's window."

"Oh, we've got to get hold of it before Saturday," said Dan. "What we'd better do, I guess, is to report it to Mr. Collins. On the face of it it's a plain case of theft, and we're not supposed to have any suspicions of Jake Hiltz."

"That's so, I guess," agreed Alf. "Perhaps Collins can scare whoever took it into giving it back. Anyhow, I've got to go home and study. Suppose you and Gerald come over after study hour and we'll find Collins and put it up to him."

"All right," Dan agreed. "But I would like to know where Hiltz spent his afternoon!"

CHAPTER XXIV
GERALD WATCHES

There was a sensation the next morning when Mr. Collins announced after Chapel that the hockey cup had disappeared from No. 28 Clarke. "It is only to be supposed," said the assistant principal, "that whoever took the cup out of the room did so as a joke. If the person will return the cup this morning, before dinner-time, I shall consider it a joke, too, although a joke in rather poor taste. If the cup is not returned by that time I shall see that the offender is punished. The Pennimore Cup is school property and there is, as you all know, a severe penalty for damaging or removing property belonging to the school. Aside from this consideration, the cup is needed to-morrow when Broadwood comes here to play hockey, and it should be the effort of every fellow to see that it is returned promptly to the office or to the manager or captain of the hockey team."

The school in general accepted the disappearance of the cup as a very excellent jest, and fellows begged each other playfully to "give it up. We know you've got it. Be good and hand it back!" But when, in the afternoon, it was learned that the missing trophy had not been returned the amusement changed to indignation. By that time Alf was thoroughly worried, and the short practice went somewhat listlessly. Gerald had seen Harry Merrow and had learned from that youth, first swearing him to secrecy, that Jake Hiltz had been on the river for at least half an hour after Gerald had stopped on the bridge. After that Harry knew nothing of Hiltz's whereabouts. Gerald reported this to Dan and Alf and Tom after practice.

"I say let's find Hiltz and put it up to him," said Dan impatiently. "We could say that he was seen in the building yesterday afternoon."

"That would be a lie, wouldn't it?" asked Tom mildly.

"Well, isn't a lie excusable in a case of this sort?" retorted Dan.

"I don't think so. You don't, either, Dan. A lie's a lie, no matter when you tell it."

"Well, what in thunder *can* we do?" Dan demanded, yielding the point without argument.

"We can't do anything," said Alf bitterly, "except wait in the hope that whoever took the cup will bring it back before the game to-morrow."

"But that's poppycock," said Dan. "If he had been going to return it he would have done it to-day before dinner and got off without trouble. Now he knows that Collins will make it hot for him. I wouldn't be surprised if we never saw that cup again!"

"Nonsense!" said Tom.

"Of course," said Gerald, "if it didn't come back dad could have another made; he'd be glad to, I know. But——"

"Meanwhile we've got to tell Broadwood that we've lost it!" interrupted Alf.

"We haven't lost it; it's been stolen," Tom corrected.

"It amounts to the same thing. We haven't got it, have we? They'll think it's a fine joke and have the laugh on us."

"Let them," said Tom. "If we beat them to-morrow I guess they can laugh all they want to."

"Maybe we won't beat them," muttered Alf discouragedly.

"Oh, buck up, Alf! Of course we'll beat them!" said Dan heartily. "Let's forget about the cup until to-morrow. There's nothing more we can do. Don't let it get on your nerves, Alf; you want to be able to play your best game, you know."

"I'm afraid it's got on my nerves already," replied Alf with an attempt at a smile. "Well, you're right, though; we've done all we can do, that's certain. Unless we find Hiltz and choke him until he 'fesses up."

"I don't believe he has it—somehow," mused Dan.

"I know he has!" said Gerald positively.

"How do you know it?" Tom demanded. But Gerald only shook his head.

Winning His "Y": A Story of School Athletics

"I just do," he answered. "I—I feel it!"

"I wish you could see it instead of feeling it," said Alf, with a laugh, as he got up. "Hang that cup, anyway! I'm going to supper. A fellow has to eat, I guess."

"I'm sure I have to," said Tom, following his example. "I've got an appetite to-night, too. I suppose that under the unfortunate circumstances I ought not to be hungry, but I am."

"So am I," said Dan quite cheerfully. "Anyway, we won't find the cup by sitting here and talking about it. I'm not going to think any more about the pesky thing. Perhaps it will show up in the morning somehow. Come on, Gerald."

"I'm not hungry," answered his roommate dolefully.

"Oh, yes, you are," said Dan laughingly. "Or you will be when you get to commons. Think of the nice hot biscuits, Gerald!"

Gerald, however, refused to be comforted and followed the others over to Whitson with lugubrious countenance. Truth, though, compels me to state that ten minutes later Gerald was doing quite well with those same hot biscuits!

Saturday morning came and the mystery of the Pennimore Cup was still unexplained. Mr. Collins made another plea for its return and threatened to expel the one who had taken it if it was not forthcoming at once. The students listened in respectful silence, but no one arose dramatically and produced the missing cup. All sorts of theories were going the rounds by now. The most popular one was to the effect that a professional thief had seen the cup in the window in Greenburg and had followed Gerald back to school and had later sneaked up to his room and stolen it. It was quite plausible and there was a general sentiment to the effect that Gerald had had a lucky escape from being robbed on the way from Greenburg, in which case he might have been killed by the desperate burglar. Few any longer believed that the cup had been taken as a practical joke, and, when dinner-time arrived and it had not appeared, even Alf and Dan and Tom abandoned their first suspicions. Only Gerald was obdurate.

"Hiltz took it," he affirmed stoutly, "and he's got it now."

And nothing any of the others could say in any way affected his conviction.

Alf gave up hoping. His dejection, however, had turned to anger, and Dan was glad to see it, since it promised better results on the rink than the captain's half-hearted, down-in-the-mouth condition of yesterday.

"As soon as the game is over," declared Alf wrathfully, "I'm going straight to the police. That's what we ought to have done yesterday morning instead of letting Collins sputter about it all this time. Maybe if we had we'd have the cup now."

"I guess we'd better tell Collins first, though," said Dan. "If the police are to be called in I suppose he'd better do it."

"Well, I'll tell him. But if he doesn't get the police I will. The whole thing's a disgrace to the school!"

The hockey game was to start at three, and an hour before that time the advance guard began to arrive from Broadwood and Greenburg. It was a glorious day, cold enough to keep the ice hard and mild enough to allow spectators to watch the game in comfort. There was scarcely a ripple of air, and what there was blew softly out of the southwest and was too kindly to bite ears or nip noses. At half past two three big coaches climbed the hill containing the Broadwood team and as many of its loyal supporters as had been able to crowd into the vehicles. Others had already arrived on foot and more followed. As it was Saturday afternoon many Greenburg enthusiasts swelled the throng of students, and long before either team appeared on the ice the rink was fringed four deep with spectators and all sorts of contrivances had been fashioned by late arrivals from which to look over the heads of those in front. French had requisitioned as many settees as he could find, and these were supplemented with boxes and planks, and finally the locker room in the gymnasium was almost denuded of its benches and would have been quite cleared had not Mr. Bendix happened along and forbidden farther spoliation.

Gerald accompanied Dan to the gymnasium when it came time to get dressed. Gerald's work was over for the season and to-day, like the members of the Second Team and its substitutes, he was only a

Winning His "Y": A Story of School Athletics

member of the audience. He hung around while the others got into their playing togs, good-naturedly helping here and there. Broadwood was dressing upstairs. When the team were ready Alf spoke to them quietly and confidently, begging them to keep together and not to sacrifice team work for individual effort. Then, clad in coats or dressing gowns, with their skates, shoes, and sticks in hand, they filed out of the gymnasium and walked down to the rink.

Their appearance was the signal for an outburst of cheers that lasted for several moments. A minute or two later they took possession of the rink and began warming up. The ice was in fine shape, hard and smooth, and the skates rang merrily as they charged up and down. Sticks clashed and pucks flew back and forth, often whizzing into the crowd and causing heads to duck. Broadwood appeared soon and received her meed of acclaim. Then for some ten minutes the teams practiced. Yardley wore white running trunks over dark blue tights, white shirts and blue knitted caps. Broadwood was attired in dark-green stockings, khaki knickerbockers, green shirts and green caps. The shirts bore, as a rule, a white B intersected by crossed hockey sticks. Of the Yardley players, five flaunted on their shirts a blue Y with a smaller H and T at right and left. At a minute or so after three the referee called the teams together and read them the usual lecture in regard to tripping, body checking, and so on. Then he tossed a coin, Alf called it, and the Blue took the north goal. The line-up was as follows:

Hanley, l. e.   r. e., Took

Goodyear, l. c.   r. c., Warner

Roeder, r. c.   l. c., Cosgrove

Durfee, r. e.   l. e., Graham

Felder, c. p.   c. p., Little

Winning His "Y": A Story of School Athletics

Loring, p.   p., Murray

Vinton, g.   g., Chisholm

Silence fell as the referee held his whistle to his lips in the center of the rink and prepared to drop the puck.

"Now, get your men, fellows, and play fast!" called Alf.

The whistle blew and the puck dropped to the ice. There was a moment's clashing of sticks and then it went back to Durfee who started along the boards with it. The enemy was on him in a moment, though, and Graham, captain of the Green, stole away with it, Durfee slashing wildly at his feet and stick.

"Cut that out, Durf!" shouted Alf. "Play the puck! Get in there, Felder, and break that up!"

Broadwood had managed to get into formation, her four big forwards strung out across the rink and skating hard, with the puck sidling back and forth from one to another. But it is one thing to reach the threshold and quite another to enter the door. Felder sent a Broadwood player spinning and Goodyear, close behind, whipped the puck away and started back with it. In a twinkling the attacked were the attackers and Yardley swung up the ice with Broadwood in hot pursuit. Across went the disk to Hanley. Took, of Broadwood, challenged unsuccessfully and Hanley passed back to Roeder, who shot. But his aim was poor and the puck banged against the boards to left of goal. There was a spirited scrimmage for its possession and finally Broadwood got away with it. After that the play stayed close to the center of the rink, neither one side nor the other being able to get by the opposing defense. Time was called frequently for off-side playing, which slowed the game up considerably.

The first score was made by Broadwood at the end of eight minutes. She had carried the puck down along the boards on the left, and Yardley had foiled her attempts to uncover long enough to shoot until the puck was past the front of the goal. Then Took evaded Goodyear and Felder and slipped the disk out in front of the cage. There was a wild mix-up for an instant and then the Broadwood sticks waved and Broadwood sympathizers shouted. The Green had drawn first blood, the puck getting past Dan's skate and lodging against the net just inside of goal.

"Never mind that!" called Alf. "Get after them. And play together, fellows!"

Yardley evened things up shortly afterwards, and there was no fluke about that score. The forwards worked the puck down to within six yards of goal and Hanley made a difficult shot from the side. In less than a minute more the Blue had scored again, Goodyear slamming the disk through from a scrimmage. Then Broadwood stiffened, and for awhile Yardley was kept busy defending her goal. Dan made some remarkable stops that wrought the audience up to a high pitch of excitement and enthusiasm, but with only a few moments to play the Green evened things up with its second tally, the puck going by Dan into the cage knee high and at such a clip that, as he said afterwards, he scarcely saw it from the time it left the ice until it was reposing coyly at the back of the net. So the first half ended with the score 2 to 2, and it was anybody's game.

The two teams seemed to be pretty evenly matched, for, although Broadwood outskated her opponent, Yardley had the better of the argument when it came to stick work. At passing Broadwood was more adept and at shooting Yardley appeared to excel, although so far she had had fewer opportunities to prove it. As the teams went off the ice Alf called to Gerald, who was standing near by:

"Say, Gerald, will you do something for me?" he asked. "I told Tom to bring that leather wristlet of mine from the room and he forgot it. Would you mind running up and getting it? You'll find it somewhere around; on the mantel, I think, or maybe on the table. This wrist of mine is as weak as anything."

"Yes, glad to," answered Gerald. "On the mantel or table, you say? And if not there, look for it, I suppose?" he added laughingly.

"Well, it's there some old place. I saw it this morning. You might look on top of the bureau. Thanks, Gerald."

Gerald hurried off up the path toward the gymnasium. He didn't want to miss any of the game, and wouldn't if he could find the wristlet and get back within the ten minutes allowed for intermission. At the gymnasium corner he cut through between that building and Merle Hall and crossed the Yard toward Dudley. He didn't meet a soul, nor was there anyone in sight. Yard and buildings were alike deserted and all the school was down at the rink.

The object of his journey wasn't found at once, for it was in none of the places mentioned by Alf. But after a minute Gerald discovered it on the floor, where it had probably dropped from the top of the bureau. He thrust it into his pocket, closed the door behind him and hurried back along the corridor. But at the entrance he stopped short and, after a moment, drew cautiously into the shadow. For across the corner of the Yard, at the farther entrance of Whitson, stood Jake Hiltz.

"What's he doing up here?" muttered Gerald to himself. "Why isn't he down at the rink? I'm sure I saw him there before the game."

Hiltz wore a long, loose ulster and appeared to be deep in a study of the sky. He stood there fully two minutes, while Gerald watched from his concealment. But while he was ostensibly regarding the heavens as though trying to decide whether it was wise to venture out without an umbrella, Gerald thought that his gaze frequently roamed to the buildings around the Yard as though to make certain that there were no eyes regarding him from the windows. At last his mind seemed to be set at rest, as far as the weather was concerned, for, with his hands thrust into his coat pockets, he stepped down from the doorway and started briskly along the path toward Dudley, whistling carelessly. And between his body and his left arm the big ulster appeared to Gerald to bulge suspiciously.

With a fast-beating heart Gerald turned and sped back and down the corridor to No. 7. Once inside he closed the door without quite latching it, crossed the room and dropped out of sight of door or windows between the two narrow beds. Then he waited.

CHAPTER XXV
THE CUP IS FOUND

"Andy, I wish you'd wrap some tape around here," said Alf, presenting his wrist to the trainer. "I sent Pennimore up for my wristlet but I guess he couldn't find it."

"Lame, is it?" asked Andy. "That'll fix it. Tell Hanley not to over-skate, cap. He missed a dozen passes last half. There you are," he added, as he snipped the end of the tape with his scissors. "Are you going to put the subs in at the end?"

"Yes, if I can, Andy. Give me the word when there's a minute or two left, will you? All right, fellows! Now let's get this game. Hanley, you've got to stop getting ahead of the line. You're missing the pass time and again. Keep back, man; take your position from Roeder and watch the puck. Durf, you've got to quit slashing with that stick or you'll be sitting on the boards; the referee's got his eye on you. Don't get ruled off, for the love of Mike! We've got all we can do to win with seven men, let alone six. Come on now and let's get this game and nail it down!"

"What's this we hear about no hockey cup, Loring?" asked the Broadwood captain, skating up as Alf jumped into the rink.

"Oh, it's a bit of mean luck, Graham," answered Alf. "Some one bagged it out of the room the other day and we haven't laid eyes on it since. We thought, of course, that some smart Aleck had taken it for a joke, but I guess now it was really stolen."

"That's hard luck," said Graham. "I'm sorry. I didn't see the cup myself, but I heard it was a dandy."

"It was. It will be all right, of course; I mean that if it doesn't turn up there'll be another to take its place, but I suppose we can't get a new one made for a month or so. I'm awfully sorry about it, and I feel rather cheap, too, having to 'fess up to you chaps that I've let it get away. If I could find the fellow who took it I'd come pretty near wringing his fool neck!"

The Broadwood captain smiled sympathetically and the referee's whistle summoned the players. The spectators, who had many of them left their positions to wander about, scurried back to the rink side. Joe Chambers searched feverishly for his notebook—for the *Scholiast* would have a full and detailed account of the game in its next issue. Harry Merrow squirmed his way to the front row between two good-natured Greenburg citizens; Tom and Paul Rand mounted their box near one corner of the rink; Andy Ryan snapped his bag shut and compared his watch with that of the timer's; Yardley and Broadwood cheered vociferously; the referee tossed the puck down between the impatient sticks and the last half began.

Up on the hill at that moment, in No. 7 Dudley, Gerald was crouching on the floor and listening anxiously for the sound of footsteps in the corridor. They came finally, drawing nearer and nearer, and at length stopping outside the door. There was a knock, then silence. Another knock, and the door swung softly inward. Cautious footsteps crossed the floor to the table. Gerald raised his head above the level of Tom's bed. Hiltz, his eyes fixed anxiously on the windows and his ears straining for sounds in the building, fumbled under his big ulster. Then the familiar maroon-colored bag appeared and he laid it on the table, the cup and base betraying their presence by muffled rattling that sounded startlingly loud in the silent room. Hiltz turned away, still listening intently, and took one step across the carpet. Then his gaze left the windows, traveled half around the room and fell full on Gerald's.

Hiltz uttered no sound, but the color fled from his face, leaving it white and drawn. His wide, startled eyes held Gerald's for a long moment. It was Gerald who finally broke the tension and the silence. He arose, brushed the dust from his knees and seated himself on Alf's bed.

"Well?" he said.

The color crept back into Hiltz's cheeks and his expression of fright gave place to one of sullen defiance.

"Well?" he echoed.

"You've brought it back," said Gerald, nodding at the cup. "I said all along that you had taken it."

"His wide, startled eyes held Gerald's for a long moment."

"I didn't take it!" said Hiltz defiantly. "I found it—just now—by accident, and——"

"Where did you find it?" asked Gerald coolly.

"In the cellar—in Whitson," replied Hiltz, after the barest instant of hesitancy.

"How did you happen to go there?" asked Gerald with a smile. "You were at the rink half an hour ago."

"I went to get something."

"Yes, and you got it, and there it is. What's the use of lying about it, Hiltz?"

Hiltz's gaze wandered to the door. Then he shrugged his shoulders and sat down in a chair by the table.

"That's right," he said. "I took it. I guess you know why."

Gerald shook his head. "I don't believe I do, Hiltz. Why?"

"To make trouble for you and Vinton, of course," answered the other recklessly. "I didn't want the old cup; I wasn't stealing it. I meant to bring it back last night and put it in your room, and I tried to, but there wasn't any chance. There were always fellows about, and after what Collins said I didn't want to be caught. I guess you've got me where you want me now, Pennimore. Of course, I might deny the whole thing," he went on musingly, "and say that you made up the story, but I guess no one would believe me."

Gerald considered judicially. Then he shook his head.

"No, I don't believe they would. You see, Hiltz, we all suspected you from the first, but we couldn't prove anything. If you ask me, I think it was a silly thing to do."

"I don't ask you," said Hiltz angrily. "I don't give a hang what you think. You don't like me and I don't like you, and you can go to Collins this minute, but I don't have to listen to any of your fool opinions."

"Why didn't you bring it back Friday morning, when you had a chance, and say that it was only a joke?" asked Gerald curiously.

"Because I wasn't ready to. You and that fool Vinton weren't worried enough then."

"I don't believe either Dan or I worried half as much as Alf did."

"Well, I'm not crazy about Alf Loring," answered Hiltz with a shrug. "He did all he could to help Vinton beat me for the committee. It was none of his business."

"Perhaps not. The only reason Dan wanted to beat you was so I could get into Cambridge. You kept me out last year, you know."

"Who said so?"

"It doesn't matter. I know it's so."

"Well, what if I did? I had a right to vote against you, hadn't I? We don't want any of your sort in Cambridge."

"My sort? Just what is my sort?" asked Gerald.

"Oh, you know; stuck-up, purse-proud chaps like you don't mix with the rest of us. You think just because your father has gobs of money that you're a little better than we are. How did he make his money, anyway?"

"Honestly," answered Gerald quietly.

"Yah! That's likely, isn't it?"

"It's so, anyhow. He didn't get it by lying and stealing, Hiltz."

"What do you mean by that?" demanded the other suspiciously.

"Well, that's what you've done, isn't it?" said Gerald. "You lied about me after the cross-country trial and now you've stolen this cup."

"I've a good mind to go over there and make you eat those words, you little stuck-up cad!" blazed Hiltz, half rising from his chair.

"I'm not afraid of you," retorted Gerald, the color rushing to his face. "You did lie when you said I cheated and you did steal that cup!"

"I didn't steal it, I tell you! I only took it to worry you fellows, and I meant to bring it back before you needed it this afternoon. And I would have if Collins hadn't threatened to expel the fellow who took it."

Gerald glanced at his watch.

"Well, I'm glad you returned it when you did," he said, "for now, if Broadwood wins, we'll be able to hand it over to her." He glanced from the cup to Hiltz and then examined his hands frowningly for a moment. Finally:

"Look here, Hiltz," he said, glancing across, "I never did anything to you personally to make you hate me so, did I?"

"Personally, no," answered Hiltz. "I'd like to see you!"

"Well, why have you got it in for me so?"

Hiltz's gaze fell and he shuffled his feet impatiently.

"Oh, I just don't like you. Tubby Jones was my best friend here until Vinton made it so hot for him he had to leave school. And then you came and took Tubby's place in No. 28, and so—" Hiltz's voice dwindled uncertainly into silence.

"I don't see what I could do about it," said Gerald with spirit. "Tubby left school because he got into some sort of trouble. That left Dan alone and he asked me to come in with him. It doesn't make much difference to me, Hiltz, whether you like me or don't like me, only—I haven't done anything to you and I'd rather not have anyone down on me if I can help it. You say I'm stuck-up, but I don't believe I am. I know there are dozens and dozens of fellows here who are smarter and nicer than I am and who haven't got wealthy fathers. Last year, when I first came here, lots of fellows used to call me names; Money-bags, and Miss Nancy, and things like that. But they don't do it this year and so I—I was thinking that they had forgotten about it and—and sort of liked me. I can't help it if my father has a lot of money, Hiltz. I don't see what that has to do with me as long as I act decently."

Hiltz was silent, his gaze fixed on his shoes.

"Do you?" asked Gerald after a moment.

"Maybe not," growled Hiltz. "I didn't say I had any very good reason for disliking you; I just said I—did." Gerald smiled and Hiltz looked up suddenly and saw it. "Oh, I know what you're after," he broke out. "You want me to eat humble pie and beg you to let me off and not tell Collins! Well, I won't, by Jove! You can go ahead and tell him now. I can stand it. Being fired isn't going to kill me."

"I don't want you to do anything of the sort," answered Gerald warmly. "I've never thought of telling Collins."

Hiltz viewed him incredulously.

"You haven't! Why not?"

"Why should I? You say I don't like you. Well, I suppose I don't. I couldn't very well after the way you've put it on me whenever you've had the chance. But I don't think I dislike you—very much. And I guess if you were decent to me I could be decent to you, Hiltz. Anyway, I'm sure I don't want you expelled."

"Then—what will you do?" asked Hiltz rather more humbly.

"Take the cup down to the rink and hand it over to French or Alf and tell them I found it in this room."

"Oh," said Hiltz, his gaze returning to his shoes. "And not say anything about me?"

"Not a word. Do you think anyone saw you come up the hill?"

"I don't believe so. I left the rink just before the first half was over and everyone was looking at the players."

"Then if I were you I'd go to my room and stay there until the fellows get back. No one will know then that you didn't stay through the game. Now I'd better take this down or the game will be over."

Gerald got up and put the cup under his arm. Hiltz arose, too, and stood hesitating doubtfully by his chair. At last:

"Well, I guess that's the best thing to do," he said. "And—oh, I guess you know how I feel about it, Pennimore. It's decent of you, I'll say that, and I—I appreciate it. My folks would feel like the dickens if Collins expelled me." He walked to the door, opened it and faced Gerald again. "I guess you and I won't—" he hesitated, hunting his words—"won't have any more trouble, Pennimore."

Then he disappeared and Gerald heard his footfalls dying away in the corridor. For a minute Gerald stood there frowning intently at the closed door. Then he smiled slightly, glanced again at his watch and left the building to hurry across the Yard and down the hill with the Pennimore cup hugged tightly under his arm.

CHAPTER XXVI
WINNING HIS "Y"

Once past the gymnasium the sounds from the rink reached him clearly; the grinding and clanging of skates, the clatter of sticks, the cries of the players and, at intervals, the savage, triumphant cheers of the onlookers. From the slope of the hill he could look over the heads of the spectators around the rink and see the skaters charging about on the ice, the blue and green costumes bright in the sunlight. Even as he looked there was a gathering of the players about the south goal, a mad moment of excitement and then the green-bladed sticks waved in air. Broadwood had scored again! Gerald wondered if that goal put the Green in the lead and hurried faster down the path.

Play had begun again before he reached the fringe of the crowd, but by the time he had wormed his way through to the substitute bench the whistle had sounded and the referee was in the center of a group of protesting players. Everyone was intent on the scene before him and Gerald's appearance went unnoticed. The referee, shaking his head, backed away, motioning, and Durfee of Yardley, and Took of Broadwood, walked disconsolately and protestingly from the rink.

"Slugging," answered Sanderson in reply to Gerald's question. "Durfee's been mixing it up all the half and Took got mad and came back at him. I don't blame him. They had a lovely little squabble down there in the corner. Didn't you see it?"

"I just got here," answered Gerald.

"Just got—" exclaimed Sanderson, looking around at him where he was leaning over the bench. "Where have you been? What's that you've got, Pennimore?"

But Gerald was trying to get Alf's attention and made no answer. Alf, finding that protests were useless, was turning to skate back to his position when he heard Gerald hail him. He looked across and then skated up to the boards.

"Did you find it?" he asked. "Thought you'd got lost. Let's have it." He began to peel the tape from his wrist.

"Yes, and I found this, too, Alf," said Gerald, bringing the cup into sight.

Alf's face lighted up when he saw it.

"Great! Where did you get it, kid?"

"Found it on the table in your room."

"All ready, Yardley?" called the referee.

"Just a minute, please," answered Alf, strapping the wristlet on. "You say you found it on the table in—" He stopped and viewed Gerald suspiciously. "How did it get there?"

"That's something I can't tell you," answered Gerald with a smile.

"Can't or won't?" asked Alf frowningly. "Well, never mind now. I've got to get back. Take the bag off it, Gerald, and don't let it out of your hands until the game's over. By Jove, I'm glad you got it, wherever it came from! You're a trump, Gerald!"

He tossed the rejected tape onto the ground and turned to skate away. But the next instant he was circling back.

"Where are your togs, kid?" he asked abruptly.

"In the gym," answered Gerald.

"Go up and get them on and hurry back!"

Then he was speeding off to his position.

Gerald stared after him. Get his togs on! Why, that meant—meant that Alf was going to let him into the game! Meant that he was to play in the big contest! Meant that he was to get his Y! For a moment he stood there motionless.

"Gee, you're in luck," said Sanderson enviously. "Why don't you get a move on, you idiot?"

Then Gerald thrust the silver cup and the ebony pedestal and the flannel bag into Andy Ryan's hands and fought his way out of the throng and went tearing up the hill.

The half was ten minutes old and a like number of minutes were left to play. Broadwood was in the lead with three goals to Yardley's two. The playing in the second period had been fairly even and the puck had been flying back and forth from one end of the rink to the other. Dan had spoiled two nice tries and the Broadwood goal had three brilliant stops to his credit. Broadwood's score had come from a scrimmage in front of the cage during which a Green forward had found a moment's opening and taken advantage of it by whizzing the puck past Dan's feet. Now Yardley braced, however, and forced the fighting. With but six men on a side the playing was more open and it was harder to penetrate the defense. Three times the Blue charged down to within scoring distance only to lose the puck. Then the penalized forwards came back into the game and Durfee, as though to make up for the lost time, sprang into the line, took the disk at a nice pass from Roeder, evaded the Green's point and slammed the puck viciously past the goal tend, tying the score again.

How Yardley shouted and cheered and pounded the boards with her feet! "Four minutes to play!" cried Ridge excitedly. "I'll bet it goes to an extra period!"

"Play together, fellows!" called Alf. "One more like that!"

Again the puck was centered and again the two teams sprang desperately into the fray. Skates rang on the hard ice, sticks clashed and broke, players stumbled and sprawled to the delight of the cheering audience, the referee whistled and interfered time and again and the precious moments flew by. Warner, the Green's right center, getting the puck near his goal took it almost alone the length of the rink amid the wild, expectant acclaim of Broadwood, sent Felder flying on his back and shot at goal. But the puck went squarely against Dan's padded leg, dropped to the ice and was whisked aside before it could be reached by the nearest green stick. Half a dozen players met in the corner of the ice and fought like maniacs for the disk. Finally it slipped out and was slashed toward the center in front of goal. But before a Broadwood player could reach it the referee's whistle sounded.

"Time's up!" was the cry along the boards. But play had been stopped only for off side and the referee motioned for the puck.

"A minute and a half, cap!" called Andy Ryan. Alf heard and waved his hand, skating across to the bench.

Winning His "Y": A Story of School Athletics

"Sanderson, you go in for Felder," he called. "Ridge at right center, Eisner at right end, Pennimore at left center. Hurry up now!"

The changes were made, the deposed players trailing regretfully from the ice to the tune of Yardley cheers.

"That's a risk, isn't it, Alf?" asked Dan anxiously, as Alf came back to position. "Putting Gerald in, I mean."

"He deserves it," answered Alf. "Keep your eyes open, Dan. There's only a minute and a half. If we can stave them off we'll have a rest and come back at them hard next period."

The puck dropped to the ice and play went on again. There was evident now a disposition on each side to abandon team work and Dan cautioned and implored almost unceasingly. Both teams were anxious to score and the result was that for the next minute neither came near doing it. Then, with less than half a minute to play, Hanley started off with the puck, pursued by the Broadwood forwards, his own mates trying desperately to get into position to help him. Down near the Green's goal the cover point challenged him and Hanley passed to the left in the hope that some one of his side would be there to take the puck. As it happened some one was there. It was Gerald, out of position and intent only on getting the disk. Two Broadwood fellows reached for it, but Gerald, skating fast, slashed their sticks aside, got the puck, lost it, recovered it again with a half turn, charged toward the cage and shot blindly. As he did so the point drove into his shoulder first. Gerald's stick flew into air and Gerald himself left his feet with a bound and went crashing to the ice ten feet away. But blue-tipped sticks were waving wildly in air and Yardley cheers were ringing triumphantly, for the puck lay snugly against the net at the back of Broadwood's goal.

Alf was the first to reach Gerald's side and his first glimpse of the pale face frightened him badly. Andy Ryan hurried on and between them Gerald was lifted up and carried off the ice and laid on the substitute's bench with a pile of sweaters under his head and a gayly hued dressing gown over his body.

"Is he hurt badly?" whispered Alf.

Andy's hands went down under the dressing gown. Then he shook his head cheerfully.

"Stunned a bit," he answered. "That's all. He hit on his head, likely. I'll look after him. You go back."

"But I've nobody to put in," said Alf.

"Play them with six," replied Andy. "There's only a matter of four seconds left."

Andy was right. The puck had no more than been put in play when the timer shouted his warning and the whistle blew. About the rink Yardley triumphed and cavorted. On the ice two weary, panting groups of players cheered each other feebly. On the substitutes' bench Gerald stirred, sighed and opened his eyes.

"Hello, Andy," he said weakly and puzzledly. "What's up?"

"I don't know what's up," answered the trainer dryly, "but you went down."

"I remember." Gerald felt of his head gingerly. "Did I——?"

He looked the rest of his question anxiously.

"You did," answered Andy. "If you don't believe me just listen to that!"

"That" was a wild tumult of Yardley joy. Gerald smiled, and when he opened his eyes again a moment later Dan and Alf were bending over him solicitously.

"How do you feel, chum?" asked Dan.

"All right," answered Gerald cheerfully. "We won, didn't we?"

"You bet! Your goal saved the day, Gerald!" answered Alf.

"And the cup," added Gerald.

"And the cup," Alf agreed smilingly.

"And—and—" Gerald's voice sank—"do I get my Y, Alf?"

"You bet you do!" answered Alf heartily.

Winning His "Y": A Story of School Athletics

"Then," murmured Gerald, closing his eyes again with a sigh and a smile, "I don't mind about my head, though it does hurt awfully!"

THE END

BY RALPH HENRY BARBOUR

The Spirit of the School
The Story of a Boy Who Works His Way through School. Illustrated in Colors. Cloth, $1.50.

Four Afloat
Four Afoot
Four in Camp

A Series of Books Relating the Adventures of Four Boy Companions. Illustrated in Colors, $1.50 each.

On Your Mark!
A Story of College Life and Athletics. Illustrated in Colors by C. M. RELYEA. 12mo. Cloth, $1.50.

No other author has caught so truly the spirit of school and college life.

The Arrival of Jimpson
Illustrated. 12mo. Cloth, $1.50.

Stories of college pranks, baseball, football, hockey, and college life.

Weatherby's Inning
A Story of College Life and Baseball. Illustrated in Colors by C. M. RELYEA. 12mo. Cloth, $1.50.

A fascinating story of college life and sport.

Behind the Line
A Story of School and Football. Illustrated by C. M. RELYEA. 12mo. Cloth, $1.50.

Captain of the Crew
Illustrated by C. M. RELYEA. 12mo. Cloth, $1.50.

A fresh, graphic, delightful story that appeals to all healthy boys and girls.

For the Honor of the School
A Story of School Life and Interscholastic Sport. Illustrated by C. M. RELYEA. 12mo. Cloth, $1.50.

The Half-Back
Illustrated by B. WEST CLINEDINST. 12mo. Cloth, $1.50.

"It is in every sense an out-and-out boys' book." — *Boston Herald*.

D. APPLETON AND COMPANY, NEW YORK

BY WALTER CAMP

Jack Hall at Yale
Illustrated in Colors, 12mo, Cloth, $1.50.

This is a story following, but not distinctly a sequel to, Mr. Camp's successful juvenile, "The Substitute." It is a story dealing principally with football in college, but including rowing and other sports. Mr. Camp's idea in this book is to give a little more of a picture of college life and the relations, friendships, enmities, etc., of the students rather than to tell nothing but a football story. In other words, the book is more of an attempt at the "Tom Brown at Rugby" idea than a purely athletic story, although the basis of the story, as in "The Substitute," is still athletics.

The Substitute
Illustrated in Colors, 12mo, Cloth, $1.50.

It describes vividly the efforts of the coaches in "whipping" the football team of a great university into shape for the season's struggles. The whole story is completely realistic—the talks of the coaches to the team; the discussion of points and tactics in the game; the details of individual positions; the daily work on the field.

Who can tell of Yale traditions, Yale ideals, and the militant Yale spirit—which the famous author has marshaled on a hundred football fields—as well as Walter Camp?

"Those interested in the great college game of football will find a most fascinating tale in 'The Substitute,' of which Walter Camp, the well-known coach and authority on the game, is the author." — *Brooklyn Eagle*.

D. APPLETON AND COMPANY, NEW YORK

BY RALPH HENRY BARBOUR

The New Boy at Hilltop
Illustrated in Colors, Ornamental Cloth Cover with Inlay in Colors, 12mo, $1.50.

The story of a boy's experiences at boarding school. The first chapter describes his arrival and reception by the others. The remaining chapters tell of his life on the football field, on the crew, his various scrapes and fights, school customs and school entertainments. His experiences are varied and cover nearly all the incidents of boarding school life.

Winning His "Y"
Illustrated in Colors, 12mo, Decorated Cloth Cover, $1.50.

The scene of this story is Yardley Hall, the school made famous in "Double Play" and "Forward Pass!"; and we meet again the manly, self-reliant Dan Vinton, his young friend Gerald Pennimore, and many others of the "old boys" whose athletic achievements and other doings have been so entertainingly chronicled by Mr. Barbour. The new story is thus slightly connected with its predecessors, but will be fully as interesting to a boy who has not read them as if it were not.

Double Play
Illustrated in Colors, 12mo, Cloth, $1.50.

Further experiences of Dan Vinton—hero of "Forward Pass!"—at Yardley Hall. He becomes in a way the mentor of the millionaire's son, Gerald Pennimore, who enters the school. There is the description of an exciting baseball game, and the stratagem by which the wily coach, Payson, puts some ginger into an overtrained squad and develops from it a winning team will appeal to every boy.

Forward Pass!
Illustrated in Colors, 12mo, Cloth, $1.50.

In his new story, Mr. Barbour returns to the field of his earlier and more successful stories, such as "The Half-Back," "Captain of the Crew," etc. The main interest in "Forward Pass!" centers about the "new" football; the story is, nevertheless, one of preparatory-school life and adventures in general. The book contains several illustrations and a number of diagrams of the "new" football plays. Mr. Barbour considers this his best story.

D. APPLETON AND COMPANY, NEW YORK

BY JOSEPH A. ALTSHELER

The Riflemen of the Ohio
Illustrated in Colors, 12mo, Cloth, $1.50.

The fourth in the series, and the best of this author's frontier Indian tales. In this story Mr. Altsheler has again conducted his now famous band of hunters and scouts over ground made historically celebrated by warfare and ambuscades in the early days of our pioneer life. The book is full of thrilling incidents and episodes, Indian seizure and torture, Indian customs in war and peace, and the graphic narration of decisive battles fought along the Ohio.

The Free Rangers
Illustrated in Colors, 12mo, Cloth, $1.50.

The exciting journey down the Mississippi to New Orleans of five young woodsmen, some of whose adventures were told in "The Forest Runners," to interview the Spanish Governor-General. After many struggles with a renegade, their old enemy, Braxton Wyatt, and a traitorous Spaniard, Alvarez, they accomplish their object and are later largely responsible for the safe voyage of a supply fleet from New Orleans to Kentucky.

The Forest Runners
Illustrated in Color, 12mo, Cloth, $1.50.

This story deals with the further adventures of the two young woodsmen in the history of Kentucky who were the heroes of "The Young Trailers." The plot describes the efforts of the boys to bring a consignment of powder to a settlement threatened by the Indians. The book is full of thrills to appeal to every boy who loves a good story.

The Young Trailers
Illustrated, 12mo, Ornamental Cloth, $1.50.

A boys' story, telling of the first settlers in Kentucky. Their pleasures and hardships, their means of protection, methods of obtaining food and ammunition are described in a way that makes the reader live with them. The life led by the young hero—his fights with Indians and his captivity among them—is vividly pictured.

The Last of the Chiefs
Illustrated in Colors, 12mo, Cloth, $1.50.

Two white boys join a caravan crossing the plains. After an ambuscade, from which they alone escape through the good will of an Indian guide, they establish themselves in the Montana hills, and live as trappers. When returning to civilization to sell their furs they are captured by Indians and witness the destruction of the tribes by Custer's army and his allies.

D. APPLETON AND COMPANY, NEW YORK

BY JAMES SHELLEY HAMILTON

Junior Days
Illustrated in Colors. Inlay in Colors on Cover, 12mo, Cloth, $1.50.

A third story by the author of "Butt Chanler, Freshman," and "The New Sophomore," in which the heroes of those stories are again in evidence with other and new characters of equal interest. In his latest story, Mr. Hamilton takes up the life of upper classmen. The story has all of the close knowledge of life at college and in a small college town that has marked Mr. Hamilton's former books, and there is also a wider and broader view befitting his older characters as they come in contact with the bigger world outside.

The New Sophomore
Illustrated in Colors. Inlay in Colors on Cover, 12mo, Cloth, $1.50.

The story of Butt Chanler's sophomore year, but with a new member of Butt's class for hero. Plot counts more than in the former story; for a strong detective interest centers around a statue of a river goddess, hidden by one class while the other attempts to find and capture it. The hero, after accidentally putting the "enemy" on the trail of the goddess, finally saves her by his ingenuity.

Butt Chanler, Freshman
Illustrated in Colors, 12mo, Decorated Cloth, $1.50.

"Butt" Chanler is a freshman, and the story begins with the first days of fall term and extending through one of the most successful baseball seasons the college has ever known. There are all the events of a freshman's life that a boy loves to look forward to and the graduate to look back upon.

D. APPLETON AND COMPANY, NEW YORK

BIOGRAPHIES FOR YOUNG READERS

Lewis Carroll
By BELLE MOSES, author of "Louisa May Alcott." A rare Portrait of Lewis Carroll as a young man as Frontispiece. Small 12mo, Cloth, $1.25 net.

This is a very charming biography of the man who wrote "Alice in Wonderland." Miss Moses, whose "Louisa May Alcott" proved so remarkably sympathetic an account of an interesting woman, has in her new book written what is, perhaps, the best and most spontaneous account ever published of a man of the most interesting personality and genius. There is more here than has ever elsewhere appeared of the younger days of Lewis Carroll, while Miss Moses's imaginative sympathy has made a most enthusiastic history of the better-known period of the career of the author of "Alice in Wonderland."

Louisa May Alcott
By BELLE MOSES. 12mo, Cloth, Illustrated, $1.25 net.

This is an admirable story of the childhood and womanhood of the celebrated author of "Little Women," told with especial reference to girl readers. Miss Moses has excellently caught the beautiful home spirit of the Alcotts's family circle, and this biography is not only charmingly written but is in every way an authoritative account of the interesting life of Miss Alcott and the New England scenes in which her days were spent. It has been Miss Moses's desire to give an intimate picture of the home life of her heroine, her development of character, and the influence upon her of the famous band of New England men and women who made Concord and Boston centers of intellectual growth.

Florence Nightingale
By LAURA E. RICHARDS. Illustrated with a Frontispiece Portrait of Miss Nightingale. 12mo, Cloth, $1.25 net.

The life of this wonderful and justly beloved woman, "The Angel of the Crimea," told by one whose father was in part responsible for confirming Miss Nightingale in her determination to devote her life to nursing. While the name of Florence Nightingale is a household word, the precise nature and scope of her work and the difficulties and discouragement under which it was accomplished are unknown to many children of the present generation.

D. APPLETON AND COMPANY, NEW YORK

Copyright © 2022 Esprios Digital Publishing. All Rights Reserved.